The thought made Glynis smile. She was not much a lady, really. Ladies did not grow up running wild in the woods, learning to shoot and skin rabbits. They did not know how to light campfires with flint, and did not dance under the full moon. They did not steal from others with guilty hearts, and they did not pose as a scoundrel's mistress.

Well, she had done what she must. She had kept her family from going hungry, or getting sick. Now her skills—and her ability to handle the Earl of St. Albans— could make the difference in helping her brother regain his title. And then she could leave this city and find a quiet village and the life that she wanted. He was the key to her brother's future—even if she had begun to realize that he might be, for her, the cause of heartbreak.

So, when Gascoyne said that the Earl waited for her downstairs, she rose and said she would dress at once and meet him in fifteen minutes.

It took twenty-five, because her maid argued with her about what she was to wear. Glynis saw no reason not to don her blue gown. It was the best she owned, and she only wore the gowns the Earl had given her when she was to be seen with him in public.

She found him waiting for her, standing quite still and staring at the clock in the hall. She bit her lower lip, then came down the stairs. "I hate being late. I am sorry."

He turned and smiled, his expression amused, the corner of his mouth quirking. "I thought you enjoyed making me wait." He took her hand. "For everything."

A MUCH COMPROMISED LADY

Shannon Donnelly

ZEBRA BOOKS
Kensington Publishing Corp.

http://www.kensingtonbooks.com

For Amy
Whose patience, good cheer, and editorial
fortitude makes this all a pleasure

ONE

His senses spun from half a bottle of brandy, but St. Albans knew that he had not drunk so much that spirits had conjured the half-naked lady in his bed. She sat upright with the white linens bunched in her fists and pulled to her chest, her hair tumbling loose and the firelight warm on bare, golden shoulders.

Anticipation quivered under the warmth of the brandy, and St. Albans realized with a shock that he could not recall the last time he had felt such an emotion. A disinterested part of him studied that question with a scholar's dispassion. But he was no scholar. And so he concentrated instead on the novelty of surprise—and the delight that reached past jaded boredom.

"One of us must be in the wrong room," he said, allowing a smile to twist up the corner of his mouth. "I do so hope it is not I."

She shook her head. A long curl of hair, as black as the shadows that clung to the corners of the sparse room, brushed across one golden shoulder. She had lovely skin. Too dark for beauty, true enough, but the dusky tones conjured thoughts of exotic lands and things foreign to English soil.

"Close the door—quickly," she said, her voice low.

St. Albans smiled. He held a woman's voice to be the most critical component of beauty, and she had a voice like wild honey, rich and deep, with an intriguing touch of refinement. This storm-soaked night had indeed improved.

From down the hall, the noise of a woman's babbling and a man's shouting carried through the inn. St. Albans was only too happy to shut the door on that racket. Then he crossed the room, his stare locked on the lush body hinted at under the bedding that she clutched to her.

It would spoil the fun if he did the mundane, so he did not ask her name. He simply walked towards her, enjoying the brandy spinning in his head and the vision of her spinning in his sight.

Her eyes glowed luminous in the dim firelight. Large and dark and endless. A softly rounded chin lifted. And a wide mouth made for indulgence edged into a smile. She did not look as if she belonged in this dilapidated room, and irritation flashed hot across St. Albans's skin. She ought to be lit by a dozen beeswax candles and draped in fine linen. Her chamber should be hung with velvet tapestries and warmed by thick rugs. A silk gown ought to caress her skin, and slide from her at his touch.

Oh, yes, she looked lady enough to be wrapped in luxury.

Instead, the room in this provincial inn halfway between Newmarket and nowhere was a shabby thing.

It was the best to be had on a soaking, late-spring night, but it was a cramped space, with the paneling scarred by age, the board floors bare and dusty, and limp, dingy curtains covering a window better suited to a monk's cell. A single rough wood chair sat before the fire, while a shaving stand huddled in the corner next to the four-poster bed, opposite a hideous maple wardrobe with carved cherubs that had long ago had their wings chipped from their plump shoulders.

It served him well enough, he had thought earlier upon being shown to the room, for traveling without his usual entourage of servants to arrange his comforts with his own linens and things about him. But now he was quite pleased not to have those encumbrances. She might not have found her way to his chamber if there had been a valet, and far too many other servants, to bar her from entry.

When he stood next to the bed, she shifted so that she sat on her knees. One slim, sun-browned hand let half the covers fall away.

His mouth dried as he glimpsed the curve of her breast, and then his lips quirked as he noticed that, under the covers, she still wore her shift and corset.

Not so daring as she wants me to think.

He wondered at what game she played. Hope flared all too briefly that it might be an interesting one. He shuttered the emotion at once. Hope was a fool's hobby, and he was no fool.

Reaching out, her long fingers deftly plucked the diamond from his cravat with a touch so light he barely noticed it. She tossed the gem onto the shaving stand with as much concern as if it were a bit of lint, and then she began to unknot his cravat. Her other hand held the covers to her breasts. He watched those tempting curves rise and fall with fast, agitated breaths. From excitement—or something else?

Stripping off his cravat, she sent it the way of his stickpin, then her slim fingers started on the buttons of his waistcoat.

She frowned as she worked at his clothes, her fingers deft and all too clever. Ah, what else could those fingers do? She bit her lower lip as she struggled with the ruby buttons—an endearing gesture that made him want to do the very same thing. She had lips that invited tasting, full and wide, plump as dark cherries.

With his waistcoat undone, she looked up, her eyes pleading. She had very dark eyes, almost as dark as the cloud of hair that curled around those warm shoulders. Gold flakes glinted in her eyes and in the strands of that dusky hair, sparkling like the dust on a jeweler's work-table. What in blazes did she want from him? Other than the obvious. And he knew for a certainty that she wanted something. What woman did not?

Normally, he cared little for the feelings of others, other than for the amusement it provided to watch them act out their follies. But she had piqued his curiosity. How delicious it was not to know exactly how this en-counter would progress. Seduction had long ago become such a predictable game. Enjoyable, but oh so predict-able.

"Your coat now," she said, her tone more urgent and her glance straying for an instant to the door.

He smiled at her naivete about gentlemen's fashions. "It generally takes two footmen to ease me out of it." Her gaze came back to him, her round chin jutting for-ward with stubborn purpose, and so he added, "But that is not going matter to you, is it?"

She rocked back on her heels, then commanded, "Turn 'round."

Her tone pricked him, and, for an instant, his eyes narrowed with a flare of anger.

No one ordered an Earl of St. Albans—not even the King, for the King was mad and the Prince Regent far too in debt to St. Albans to do more than be grateful for the discreet loans that kept the Prince in luxuries.

She shrank back a little before him, and he forced his cursed temper to cool. He had not drunk so much as to lose control of himself. He never drank so much. And he was not about to forfeit this delicious, dusky lady by frightening her with the dark edge of his own damnable self.

Besides, she was indeed giving him a full night of novelties. When was the last time anyone had dared order him to do anything? So, where he defied princes, he would obey her. For now.

Giving her one of his better smiles—the one calculated to charm any woman—he turned. "Will this do?" he said, allowing only the slightest of sarcasm to shade his tone. Then he waited to see what she might dare next.

Her breath, hot and sweet, teased the back of his neck as she reached around him to grasp his coat collar. Her breasts brushed his back, then she pulled away to strip his coat down so that it pinned his arms. Panting and muttering curses in a tongue he did not recognize, she peeled the garment off and tossed it aside as if it were a rag. His waistcoat went with it, and the ruby buttons winked up at him like demon eyes.

He spared a brief regret for his coat, which now lay in a wrinkled, ruined heap. He had rather liked that particular shade of midnight blue, but he could get another. Naked ladies—at least those this comely and intriguing—were rather more hard to come by.

In his shirtsleeves and pantaloons now, he decided he had done with what she wanted.

He turned in an instant, catching her in his arms. Feeling her stiffen and hearing her gasp, he carried her down with him, falling into the depths of the feather mattress so that she lay trapped beneath him.

The sheets, worn to threads, tore under them as his hands tangled in her hair and her garments and the bed linens. She smelled of wild roses and some spice that stirred his pulse. Her shift dragged lower onto her shoulders. Against her low-riding corset, her breasts rose and fell with rapid breaths that feathered across his face. Her pulse skittered in her throat, and her hands pressed up against his chest, fingers splayed wide, as if somehow that would stay him for even a moment.

He smiled down at her. They were now firmly in his domain and he would dictate the rest of the night.

"Now, my sweet intrigue. Time to see if you strip as well as you strip me."

Eyes enormous and flashing, she pushed against him, muttering something in that foreign tongue of hers. He did not understand the words, but a curse was a curse in any language. He smiled at her protests. They would not last for long. Then he lowered his mouth to hers.

A pounding cut across his intent and he hesitated, a frown tightening his face. He started to turn towards the door and the noise, but the lady's fingers wrapped into his lawn shirt. Then she dragged his mouth down to hers.

He forgot the pounding outside for the pounding inside as blood coursed through him, hot and heavy and leaving him light-headed. He had no room in his mind for anything but the beseeching demands being made.

Her teeth bit at his lower lip, then her tongue soothed what she had bitten. Twenty years of practiced seductions vanished in a hot flash of raw desire, going up like dry powder touched by a spark. He fit his mouth over hers, demanding more, devouring her, tasting every curve of lip and tongue, exploring every hollow and probing until he pulled a soft moan from her.

Closing his hand over her breast, he released her mouth and sought the taste of the skin on her neck, on her throat, on the valley between her breasts. She sighed, or was it a ragged pull of breath? And then the door crashed open behind them.

The lady squeaked and dove under the tousled covers, wiggling out from his loosened hold.

St. Albans growled, anger cooling his passion of a moment ago. Slowly, he rose on one elbow, his movements measured and intentionally languid so that his controlled moves kept his temper at least somewhat in check. With the pulse pounding in his clenched jaw, he locked a narrowed stare on the intruders.

Three men crowded the threshold. St. Albans inspected them. An aged, balding, scrawny fellow—the landlord. A vacant-eyed young edition of him—the son. And a gentleman in a purple coat, his face pinched and lined, his silver hair worn long and tied back in the style of the last century, with a too-fastidious air about him.

St. Albans recognized him at once, but he took the course of deliberately insulting the man by not acknowledging that fact. After all, facts had never mattered to an Earl of St. Albans. And he had a personal dislike for Francis Dawes, Lord Nevin. There was still a score to settle between them.

For a long moment, St. Albans simply stared at the trio, his fury at this interruption quivering inside him. He sent the unspoken message quite clearly to them: if he had to rise, they would regret it. Deeply.

The landlord, in a nightshift hastily stuffed into half-buttoned breeches, glanced about wide-eyed, taking in the scene, then stuttered and began to bow himself out. Lord Nevin ignored him, pushing forward as if this were his house and he carried the authority here.

Conceited, overbearing hypocrite, St. Albans thought, his patience with this farce thinning.

"There's a thief loose," Nevin said, his narrow face pulled tight as he stared down at St. Albans with disdain. "We are searching all the rooms."

St. Albans half expected the man to drag out a handkerchief and put it to his face, as if he smelled something offensive. Instead, Nevin gestured for the landlord and his son to move forward.

With the smallest of movements, St. Albans turned his stare to the landlord and asked in a deadly sweet voice, "Do you mean to accuse me of harboring a fugitive?"

A chorus of denial burst from the landlord and his

son. both men shifted nervously on their feet, glancing from St. Albans to Nevin.

"Then why do you enter my room, startling my lady?" St. Albans asked, his voice softening as his anger began to fade. Interruptions were always such bores.

"A Gypsy girl broke into my rooms," Nevin said, red-faced now, his small mouth pulled down and the lines that bracketed his lips deepened with determination. "I will have her caught and up before the law."

He came forward a step, an emerald ring flashing fire on his left forefinger as he moved.

"You certainly will not if you are dead, sir."

The older man hesitated, uncertainty clouding his gray eyes. "Dead? Is that a threat, you . . . you . . ."

"That, sir, is plain speaking. My usual habit for dealing with intruders is to shoot them. So far, I have made an exception in your case out of consideration for the lady. However, my consideration for anyone has its limits."

Nevin huffed as if he did not believe this, but he also did not take another step forward.

Watching the fellow, St. Albans wondered if perhaps Nevin had not heard that the Earl of St. Albans never bluffed. Their paths in Society crossed little enough that Nevin might be unaware of anything more than the gossip—most of it true—that St. Albans had shot three men. One in a fair duel, and the other two not. Just in case, St. Albans shifted.

Moving his hand out from under the lady beside him, he slid it under his pillow. However, his fingers did not find the curve of his pocket pistol. He felt nothing. No smooth mahogany stock. No chill of silver filigree. Just bare, worn bed linen.

Annoyance flared again inside him, and then quickly died as the novelty of the situation caught his fancy. So the lady in his bed had no use for diamond stickpins, but she had one for loaded pistols. He could not help the quirk that lifted the corner of his mouth. Oh, she really was a delight. He simply could not afford to let these louts ruin his evening with her.

"Get out," he said, already starting to turn back to where she cowered under the covers with only her dark curls peeking out from the bed linen.

A hissed curse came from Nevin, but the landlord was already muttering about how the thief must have slipped down the back stairs, and those Gypsies were probably already miles down the road.

Hearing the desperation to leave in the man's voice, St. Albans glanced back at the trio. "Oh, go find your own woman elsewhere, Nevin. And leave me mine."

Fury blazed in the older man's eyes. His mouth pulled into a tighter sneer. "You . . . you disgust me."

"Oh, for . . . Go and be disgusted elsewhere, unless it is that you have a fonder taste for watching sin."

Nevin glanced once more at the form concealed by the covers. The emerald glinted again as his fingers clenched, then loosened. Stiffening, he swung around and strode out, his back stiff.

The landlord began another set of ducking bows, pushed his gawking, sleepy son out before him, and then left, pulling the door shut behind him.

St. Albans waited until he heard the click of the broken latch, then he swung out of bed. Dragging the wooden chair forward, he secured the chair-back under the knob.

Then he turned back to the bed.

As he had expected, his Gypsy had sat up again and now she pointed his own pistol at his heart. The silver glinted in the firelight as her slim hands quivered with the faintest tremble. It was very faint, but enough to make him cautious. His pistol had a rather light trigger, and he did not care to tempt a nervous woman. It would probably be a blessing to the world if she shot him dead, but odds were that she'd only maim, and he had seen just how cursed painful a bullet could be.

No. That fate did not interest him.

Crossing his arms, he leaned against the wall. "My dear delight, pray do not spoil the evening by becoming predictable. A shot will only bring them back, and you can hardly want that beautiful neck of yours ruined with a hangman's rope. Besides, I can entertain you far better alive than I can dead."

Her wide mouth pulled down, and then she said in that teasingly cultured, throaty voice, "I do not have to kill you—only wound you."

He smiled. "You had best aim to kill, sweet desire. I honestly do have the devil's temper, and unless you shoot me dead, I cannot vow to show you anything but my worst side."

Glynis hesitated. The grim certainty in his tone sent a shiver along her skin. She did not want to see his worst side. She did not think she would care much for it. And she did not want to shoot him. She did not want to shoot anyone, in fact. Drat him for being right, anyway. A pistol report would only bring back the others. She ought to have heeded the cards. But if she had not come, Christo would have. And he had not her light touch, so it had had to be her.

At least she had seen the box. As they had heard, Francis Dawes traveled with it, keeping it close to him. She had almost touched the dragon carved upon it, but she had had no time to do more. So now she must get back to Christo and lay new plans. Better plans.

Only this green-eyed devil stood in her way.

Lowering the pistol, she eyed him cautiously. She kept her fingers wrapped tight around the cool feel of polished, deadly wood. She did not trust this *gaujo*, with his steady gaze that seemed to look into her, and his cold voice, and his too-hot touch. Her lips still tingled from that kiss he had taken. Of course, she had offered herself. She had to own that. But she had not expected what had followed.

Thinking only to befuddle him, and to hide herself, she had pulled him to her. And then a storm of fire had swept her into a spinning world of heat and sensation. He had done that to her. How? How did he know how to do such things to a woman?

She studied him, as if viewing a new kind of wild animal.

He had the conceit of his kind, this *gaujo* lord. It was bred into the clean, sharp lines of his jaw and cheekbone, and that arrogant nose. It lay coiled in the wide shoulders and strong muscles now exposed by his disordered shirt and his close-fitting pantaloons which outlined every lean sinew. There was much to interest a woman. But also much she despised. He stood there as if he owned this room and all in it—her included. His eyes were as cool as any green glen, and she knew how easy it was to hide danger in such places.

As she studied him, his smile twisted his mouth into a cynical slant. He had a sensuous lower lip, full and soft. Her pulse galloped faster as tension crackled in the air. She knew how that mouth had felt on her. And how his hair, drawn into glinting gold by the firelight, had felt like the finest silk fringe under her fingers.

No, she did not trust this *gaujo*.

So she kept hold of the pistol, but she put on her best pleading face, the one she used for begging shelter on someone else's land. "Please . . . please, let me go. I stole nothing."

One eyebrow lifted in such mockery that her fingers itched to shoot him for no better reason than to obliterate that look from his face and replace it with shocked surprise. His eyes, however, warmed as they rested on her, and the appreciation in them cooled her temper, though it did nothing to make her feel more comfortable.

"You mean, rather, you came away empty-handed. Come, my delight, be honest at least. You may not be a thief, but it is not from lack of trying."

Her temper flared and her chin shot up. "You mean I am a Gypsy, so I must be a thief! Well, I came looking only for what is rightfully mine. For what that lying *gaujo* stole from me—from my family!"

"Gaujo? And what is a *gaujo?"*

Struggling to temper her pride, she tried to remember the lessons her mother had taught. *Surrounded by the Gadje, the Rom's only defense is his tongue.*

She shifted on the bed, and his gaze flickered over her body. She had a far better weapon there than any mere pistol. But she would have to take care how she used it.

Softening her tone, she said, "You're *gaujo.* As was that other lord. It is someone who is not one of the traveling people."

"Well, that is true enough, but I do object to being classified with Nevin. We really do not have much in common—other than perhaps an interest in you." A measuring look came into his eyes. "And I will point out that you did steal one thing—my pistol."

She glanced down at the silver-and-wood pistol that lay in her hand. It would fetch a goodly price in any market, and Bado would certainly have urged her to pocket it—and the man's gems—for the good of the family. But she hated that such need had always driven her.

Looking up at this *gaujo* again from under her eyelashes, she saw his mocking smile, and she could not bear it. She had too many times been called thief—justly and unjustly. Well, no more. She had sworn that day when *Dej* had told them of their true inheritance that there would be only one thing for which she used her skills. By God she had sworn, and on her father's memory. She would not break that vow.

Slowly, carefully, she put the pistol on the pillow beside her. Then, rocking back on her heels, she folded her hands in her lap.

"I have stolen nothing," she said, her expression kept empty. There, let him try to do what he wanted with her. She knew a few tricks yet to deal with such as him.

St. Albans's pulse kicked up a notch. Such an unwise move for her to relinquish her protection. He could now put her back where he wanted her—underneath him.

And yet he stood there, arms crossed, not moving towards her. Oh, damn his curiosity. It would indeed be the death of him one of these days.

"If you are not a thief, then why are you here? What did he take from you that you would risk your neck to get it back?"

Tilting her head, she studied him from the corner of her dark eyes. *What lie will she tell me?* he wondered.

Then she said, her voice credibly even and her gaze steady. "I was his mistress. He promised me a box of jewels, and I came to claim that from him."

St. Albans's mouth quirked. Oh, she really was quite wickedly wonderful. Liar, thief, and Lucifer knew what else. Virtue had always attracted him with its fascinating illusion, but sin had always been far more entertaining.

"You were his mistress?" he repeated. He knew enough of Nevin to know that the man would never take any creature so low as a Gypsy to his bed—no matter how tempting. Thank heavens he himself had no such prejudice.

She frowned at him, those dark eyes flashing.

"And he promised you a box of jewels?" St. Albans said, hoping to prompt her to embroider her story.

Slowly, she nodded. His smile widened, and Glynis's heart began to hammer a warning again.

Uncrossing his arms, he pushed off the door and came towards her. She forced herself to sit still and watch him approach. She knew better than to flinch. A hound always chases the fox who runs. Better to hold still, then dodge at the last moment, if she could.

"In that case, my delight, forget Nevin. I shall give you far more than a box of jewels."

She waited until he reached the bedside and then she scurried back, putting the width of the bed between them. She had no illusion of safety. She had felt the strength in his arms. But all she needed was to stay away from his reach, and to find a way to unblock the door.

"Do you think me a fool to believe such a promise again? You are like him. You will say anything now, but come the morning, you will give nothing."

Green fire flashed in his eyes. Glynis's throat tightened and her pulse skittered. She knew how dangerous it might be to taunt a lord such as him, and now she saw just how much he hated to be compared to Francis Dawes.

"You dare . . ." he started to say, and then cut off his words. He pressed his mouth tight, so that his upper lip thinned to a cruel line. And then his mouth softened and quirked. "You are good. Very good, indeed. A lie to feint, and then a *botta segrete* to score a palpable hit."

She frowned. "I don't understand."

"Fencing, my delight. A secret attack. You compare me to Nevin, hoping I shall respond and offer you an opening. And almost I did. But the wound is not fatal, my Gypsy, and I did warn you that you had best go in for a kill."

He smiled and began to move around the bed.

Panic flooded Glynis. She thought briefly of trying to scramble across the bed for the door, but instincts tingled, warning her that he wanted her tangled in those covers again. Well, she would not play his game. She had no hope of winning.

Backing into the corner, she watched him come around the end of the bed until he stood before her, the fire lighting one side of his face and the other half of him in shadows. Heat blazed from his skin, far warmer than the embers in the fireplace. She wet her lips and swallowed, but her throat remained hollow and parched. Her heart pounded faster against her ribs, and she struggled to keep her mind clear and quick.

"You are right," she admitted. "That was a lie. And you deserve better, for you did not give me away to the others and I see now that you could have. You are not like that man. You have honor in you."

He stopped his advance and stared down at her, his expression startled and a little bemused. "Honor? My dear, you really did choose the wrong room for hiding if you think that."

"No. I chose well. I heard the maids talk of you—that you like women. And so I knew that you would be a good man." She gave him a warm smile. "After all, how can any man who likes women not be good in his heart?"

St. Albans stared at her, baffled and distracted. Her logic defied rationality. It also irritated him. What in blazes was he doing arguing philosophy with her? And yet, he could not let these delusions of hers persist. "My sweet mystery, a love of the fair sex is the least likely indication of virtue in this world."

Still smiling, she shook her head, her eyes wide and staring up at him with such trust that he started to feel not only annoyed with her, but with himself. Be damned, but was this a seduction or an argument about his black soul? Oh, he had had enough of this.

Before he could move, however, she spoke, sealing his fate. "But do you wish to hear the whole of how I came to choose you to protect me?"

Two

No, I don't want to hear this, he told himself. Only the truth was that he rather did want to hear it. The very idea that anyone could view him as a savior amused him no end, for he always had been on the opposite side of such protection, from gentlemen looking after their daughters, their wives, and even their mistresses. Curiosity itched inside him, meaning that he could not simply sweep her into his arms and kiss her silent.

She will only lie again, he told himself.

However, he wanted to hear the next invention that would come from those delectable lips.

With a sigh of resignation, he crossed his arms again, hoping that would seem less threatening to her, but ready to pounce should she try to slip past. Then he leaned his shoulder against the wall. She must be playing for time. But he was a good enough angler to know that the real sport lay in the art of allowing the fish to run when it would. For now, it amused him enough to watch her play his line.

"Why do I have the feeling this is a long story?" he asked.

She gave a small shrug. "Your part in it is not, which is all that would interest you."

His mouth quirked. "What, did the maids also fill your ears with stories of my being a vain fellow, attentive only to myself?"

"No. That I have seen for myself tonight."

"Oh, you do have a sharp edge to your tongue. But I assure you that I can actually manage to be engaged by a number of things outside my own self. But, my own ease does come first, so if this is going to be a very long—"

"Only long enough."

"We still ought to be comfortable." He swept his arm around the barren room. "I would offer you a chair, only it is otherwise occupied, so you shall have to make do with the bed. Oh, you may save your suspicious glances. My bite is generally regarded by ladies as considerably nicer than my bark."

St. Albans allowed his smile to warm, calculating the exact amount of charm to exert. It always amazed him that people were so easily disarmed by a mere curving of the lips.

She, however, did not seem inclined to be easy. With a scornful glance at the bed, she threw wide her arms, her face expressive and her eyes bright with indignation. "How can I sit and tell you my *swato*—my story? Bah! That is no good. I need to show you as much as tell you!"

She was up to something, right enough. She wanted out from her corner, and this was but an excuse to get past him. He knew it as well as he knew his own name. But, despite his certainty that she was plotting something, he wanted to hear this *swato* of hers. Besides, she could not get past the door without moving the chair. And he rather liked how those gestures did interesting things with those lush curves of hers.

Uncrossing his arms, he gave her a courtly bow and offered room for her to step past. She gave him a side-long glance, and he decided if she gave him many more of those looks from under those thick, dark lashes, he would not be able to allow her to finish her story without ravishing her. But then she scooted past him, her fast step betraying her nervousness, and he thought that this was far more entertaining than an ordinary seduction.

He followed her around the foot of the bed, then seated himself on the rumpled linens. After sliding his pistol back to its place under the pillow, he shifted on the bed to face her.

She had pulled up the sleeves of her shift so that the thin fabric covered her shoulders, but in her underclothes and with her hair rumpled she looked as if she had already been deliciously tumbled. The firelight warmed her face, casting a glow onto her high cheekbones and that round chin of hers.

He lay back, propping himself up on one elbow. "So what is this . . . this *swato* of yours?"

Glynis settled her hands on her hips, and forced her smile back in place. She had the door to her back, and everything inside her screamed to turn and run. But the chair under the doorknob would slow her too much. And her dress and cloak still lay underneath this *gaujo's* bed, where she had stuffed them after slipping into his room. What a mistake she had made there, but no use came of regret. She needed a new plan now, and time enough to think of it.

So, wetting her lips, she began talking.

As with any good *swato* there was some truth. She owed him that much for not betraying her earlier. But a *swato* needed a little fantasy, too. And she had Christo and *Dej* to protect. She could not risk betraying their presence nearby.

So she told him how she came to the inn after hearing that a man who went by the title Lord Nevin was staying there. Happy to have their fortunes told, the maids had let her into the kitchen, but they told her more than she ever revealed to them. That was the usual way of it. Her *dej* had taught her well to tell fortunes from the questions asked. But now Glynis could see why one girl had giggled nervously, and another had asked with apprehension if she would catch the eye of the wicked Earl of St. Albans.

Seeing him as he was now—sprawled elegantly across the bed, looking as boneless and lazy as a cat, his green eyes large and glittering with intriguing lights—she could believe those stories the tavern maids had told her. She had thought they must be elaborating that he was the most depraved rake in England—a gentleman by title only, and a man to fear and avoid. They had said that he took any woman he wanted, that he gambled and drank and did what he pleased. That he was a dangerous man.

For he could make any woman love him.

She had almost laughed at their words.

But now she could see how he could do just such a thing.

He had skin that glowed like rich butter. She had never seen such skin before on a man. Peeking from the 'V' made by his white shirt, the hair on his chest caught the light and tempted like strands of gold. Almost she wanted to touch it, to stroke the muscles she glimpsed there. That would be about as safe as stroking a steel trap.

Yes, he looked like a trap ready to spring. He concealed the tension coiled inside him with languid grace, but her *dej* had taught her well. *Dik and shoon*—watch and listen, Mother had always said, though her mother's own eyes were now sightless.

So Glynis watched this one as she spoke, and what she saw kept her heart pounding and her nerves stretched tight.

Stalling for more time, she told how she had slipped upstairs when the maids had left to answer a summons back to work. She did not tell him how she had gotten past a locked door—he had no need to know about her skills in such matters. However, the knowing glint in his eyes as she slipped past this point made her squirm in her own skin. He seemed to know far more than she told him. She did not like that. It made him seem more Romany than *gaujo,* and she liked better to think of him as an arrogant, hateful *gaujo* lord.

With luck, she would soon be gone from here and never see him again.

Only why did her heart twist a little at that thought? Oh, he was a devil to smile at her with his eyes. To stare at her with warmth in his gaze. To lie so very still that she began to forget her fear of him.

She needed more than luck tonight. She needed all her wits and cunning, or her escape from him might cost her dearly.

She forced a wider smile. "You were clever to sense my lie—I was never mistress to Lord Nevin. But that one, he holds papers that he carries inside a box that are mine. One of the maids came to his room and found me before I could take it. I slipped away, but the girl cried thief. So I ran."

One golden-brown eyebrow rose. "Into my room, where you could pose as my doxy for the night? You do like high-stake games."

She had to agree with him on that. Only he had no idea just how high the stakes were.

He went on, his voice lazy. "But what papers could Nevin possibly have that you would want? You are leaving out some rather important details here."

She lifted one shoulder and her shift slipped distractingly lower. St. Albans watched her push it back up and decided that he was going to enjoy pulling it down again.

Then she raised her chin and looked him straight in the eye, her stare unblinking. "Those papers are marriage lines that would prove the truth of marriage to Lord Nevin's son."

St. Albans held utterly still. Disbelief, icy and raw, trickled into him. Married? Her? To Nevin's son? No. It was preposterous. It ought not to matter, but it did. He did not want his Gypsy owned by Nevin's son. Or anyone else. His glance slid over her, and a confused anger beat hot and heavy against his chest. Pushing down the emotion, he tried to think.

It must be a lie. Did Nevin even have a son? He recalled vague talk of one. Yes, an heir. At university still, he rather thought, so that would put the son at about her age. But it could not be. Nevin was far too high in the instep to allow his own blood to marry so far beneath him. The man even had the effrontery to think his lineage surpassed all others, for its purity of Norman blood. But the earls of St. Albans had been Saxon lords long before Nevin's kin arrived on these shores.

However, that was not the topic at hand. No, it was this ludicrous idea of a marriage between his Gypsy and . . .

No. He would simply not allow it to be.

He relaxed again, but his eyes narrowed as he saw the flaw in her lie. "There is but one obvious question, my sweet, which is why, if these papers are in Nevin's reach, does he not destroy them?"

Arching an eyebrow, she shot him an irritated look as if he were a simpleton. "He has the box, not the papers. And he does not know the trick to the secret bottom that is concealed there. Lord Nevin's son hid them there for safekeeping, but if they are found and destroyed . . ."

Her face paled and her mouth tightened, and the certainty flooded St. Albans that she meant every word she spoke. But it all seemed too dramatic, with this talk of secret compartments and marriages. Dramatic, but plausible.

"I have vowed to get those papers, and I shall. On my father's memory, I will get them back."

"And what if I said I would get them back for you?" he asked.

Surprised by himself, he wondered briefly where that offer had sprung from. Of course he had no intention on making good on such a promise. It was not even yet a promise, merely a question. But he did hope that she would now try to use her charms to persuade him to assist her.

However, she did not look as if she contemplated any such persuasion. Folding her arms, she studied him, her mouth pulled down and a skeptical, assessing look in her eyes.

"You? What could you do?"

For a moment, he thought that he must not have heard her correctly, and then her words sank in.

What could you do?

The scorn in her tone stung like a wasp's barb. Of all the . . . Why, the insolent little baggage! Who the deuce did she think she was speaking to? Some . . . some upstart baronet?

Rolling off the bed, onto his feet, he stalked towards her.

She fell back, her hands falling loose to her sides and then sliding behind her. Her eyes widened, as if she had only just realized her mistake.

A too sizable mistake, he thought, his temper barely in check.

"My sweet misguided Gypsy, either you failed to gain enough information from these tavern wenches, or you have not quite grasped my identity."

Glaring up at him, she stopped backing up and stood her ground. He stopped before her, so close that he could feel her anger flare in an almost tangible aura of heat.

"Oh, I know exactly who you are! I see your kind every day. A *gaujo* who thinks too much of himself, who has too much time to find himself trouble, and whose idea of help for anyone is to offer money. Well, keep your coins, *gaujo*. Some of us work for what we want!"

His fist bunched and he only just stopped himself from taking that elegant neck in his hands to throttle her. No one, but no one, spoke to him in that tone of voice. And no one had the right to criticize him.

Keeping his own voice very even and low, he told her, just so that she would be quite clear and not make this mistake again, "My dear Gypsy, I am Simon Alexander Derain Winters, Earl of St. Albans, Baron Winters, Baron of Wexford and Fleet, Knight of the Garter, and there is damn little I cannot do if I so please, including get away with murder. Which I shall be happy to prove to you should you insist on continuing this most unwise discussion. And if you call thieving work, then no wonder you have such a misguided view of the world and my place in it."

Her glance dropped and thick lashes fluttered low, but then she looked up again, her dark eyes burning, the gold in them glinting hot as coals. However, uncertainty also shadowed those eyes.

Under his abraded pride, regret stirred. In truth, he did have too much time for trouble, and he did solve a good many problems with coin. Had he not just been thinking of how much she might cost him? However, that was not, he told himself, what he had meant when he had asked what he might do for her.

Blast her, but he would not be acting so badly if she had not started this all by asking him what could he do.

He was the Earl of St. Albans. Had been from the day he was born, since his father had been wise enough to break his neck. He could do anything he pleased.

And he was not, he thought with gritted teeth, going to listen to the laughter of those ghosts from his past; those things he could not do were things he chose not to. And that was that.

He turned his mind from those ancient losses, but those shadows tempered his mood. She did not know him. And he should not be so angry with her for being ignorant. Indeed, it was part of her charm that she did not know him well enough to be cautious.

"You may apologize now, my sweets," he said, trying hard to soften his tone. Reaching up, he brushed a dark curl from her cheek. "And then we shall move on to more pleasant things."

His finger brushed across her skin, warm and tender. And Glynis's fear vanished like a fire doused by sand. She struggled to find the armor of her anger, but too many emotions had buffeted her tonight. Too much fear, too much of nerves strung tight, too much scorn. She just wanted it over. Fatigue filled her bones and weighted her soul, and she knew suddenly that she was done fighting her own fate.

She had thought mention of marriage might make him lose interest. He had not. She had thought that if she gave him a shrewish tongue, that would put him off. It had not. And she saw now that she would have to pay the price for the mistake of putting herself into his path.

"Oh, just have done with it," she told him. Then she shut her eyes tight and turned her face to him, prepared to endure his kiss, and whatever would follow. He would take what he wanted from her, and then she would just have to hope that no child came from this. If it did, she would deal with that, too. She had dealt with so much already in life. What was one more set of burdens?

Staring at the woman before him, the image that St. Albans had tried to blot out for the past six months rose again. The vision flashed in his mind of a golden-haired beauty—the only woman he had ever allowed to escape. And that good deed had done nothing but torment him. What idiot had ever said that virtue was a reward? It had become a blasted curse.

For six months, he had tried to obliterate the uncomfortable feelings that that one act had stirred within him. So what if that lady had seemed to find love with another? Love never lasted. And that lady and her lord were merely fools, living in a delusion that would shatter someday. Of course, they made London a boring place to be, for at any moment the pair of them might turn up to remind him that he had given in to that idiotic impulse; he had told that lady the truth instead of seducing her into staying with him.

His reward had been nothing but a restless unease that he could not shake.

Ah, those fools would be the ones who someday regretted their folly. But he was bloody well not going to allow the sight of them—happy as only the besotted can be—to ruin his pleasure.

Which is why he was not in London.

Taking his Gypsy's chin in his fingers, he tilted her face up. This one, he would not let go. Not even if she turned to wood in his arms. He had learned better of himself. He would take what she offered, and enjoy it, and he would bloody well make her enjoy it as well.

He began to lower his lips towards hers, and then stopped when his mouth hovered a breath away from hers.

Staring down at her closed eyes, he told her, "I mean to have you no matter what."

He felt her chin move as her throat contracted. Then she said, "So have done. And then I will go."

"What if I don't want to let you go after?"

Her eyes opened then, wide and alarmed. He smiled. Ah, at last. Better to have her scratching like a wildcat than stiff with martyred submission.

However, the alarm vanished from her eyes, and she smiled. His senses sharpened with warning. What was she planning now? He waited, relief washing through him that she was no blond, blue-eyed innocent. Heaven and Hades save him from such ladies ever again. Far better to have this dark-eyed Gypsy full of too many inventive ideas, a little liar and a thief, and fair match for his own dark soul.

She wet her upper lip with her tongue, then said, "Perhaps then we shall talk more about your helping me—if I help you beforehand?"

St. Albans leaned forward to capture that mouth with his, but a firm hand on his chest stayed him.

"I said *perhaps*. But do you not wish me to first help you from your other clothes?"

He eyed her warily, but then she tugged his shirt loose from his pantaloons and smoothed a hand over his stomach and up his chest. Pinpoints of pleasure danced through him.

"Whatever did you have in mind?" he asked with a smile.

"A game. A Gypsy game. You must stand in the middle of the room with your eyes closed. And for every garment I take off, you must take off one, as well. But there is one thing—you must not open your eyes until I tell you to. It is bad luck, and I will never trust you if you promise not to look and then do so before I tell you."

She was at it again. Scheming. He glanced at the chair propped under the doorknob. She could not move it without his hearing the scrape of wood on wood.

So why not indulge her?

"Where do want me to stand?" he asked.

She led him to a spot halfway between the bed and the door, then asked him to close his eyes. The smile she gave him as she spoke had his pulse hammering.

"Promise not to look before I say," she told him, her mouth pulling into a pout.

"I promise."

"No, it must be a sacred vow. On your honor."

"I have little enough of that, my sweets."

"Then on your family's name."

"Oh, very well. I promise, on the name of Winters that you have the word of the Earl of St. Albans not to look before you say."

Her hand brushed his chest again, leaving his skin tingling. He closed his eyes and was rewarded with the sound of cloth rustling, then stiff fabric was draped across his naked shoulder.

"That is my corset. Now, in turn, pull off your shirt. But keep your eyes closed."

He obeyed, and began to think that he could actually become accustomed to such commands from her. For a time, at least. Perhaps he would even keep her with him for a few days or so. It had been long enough, after all, since he had had any such lengthy liaison.

More cloth rustled, then soft fabric lay across his shoulder and her voice whispered in his ear, "There is my shift. Now I have nothing on at all. Will you match me before I tell you that you can look?"

It took a few moments for him to strip off his pantaloons. Knitted from fine wool, they clung to his legs, but he soon dragged them off and tossed them aside. He did not wear any drawers underneath, and the cool air swirled around his bare skin.

Straightening, he waited a moment for her next command. What would she do before she told him to open his eyes? He liked how resourceful she was. Perhaps they might even enjoy each other's company a few weeks?

The silence lengthened. Tilting his head, he stretched out his other senses. He had not heard the chair scrape, so she must still be in the room—and yet, it was too quiet. Too empty.

A cold draft wound around his legs.

Opening his eyes, he spun around.

She was gone.

He stood naked in an empty room. The chair stood on its four legs beside an open doorway. Fury pulsed so hot in his veins that he almost forgot his lack of dress and went after her. Then cold air began to cool his body and his head. He glanced down at his naked skin and a smile lifted one side of his mouth.

That little witch. So, she thought she had made good her escape. She thought this was done.

Well, she had not yet learned what it was to deal with the Earl of St. Albans.

Glynis ran down the backstairs of the inn, her bare feet slapping quietly on the wood. The door creaked as she pushed it open, but the noise of the taproom muffled the sound. Under her cloak, the cold swirled up and chilled her skin as she slipped outside. She winced as her feet slipped into mud. A pity she had to leave her shoes under that *gaujo's* bed, but she knew when to cut her losses. At least the rain had stopped. The air smelled wet and sharp with the sweetness of early roses and the earthy pong of the stables that lay behind the inn. Overhead, clouds danced, parting to reveal the silver splinter of a new moon, and then closing again to hide its glow.

Clutching her dress to her naked body, Glynis tightened her hold on her cloak and ran through the squishing mud. She had no regret for her shift and her corset. They were small payment to make. But her dress was of good wool, and with only three dresses to her name she had risked the few seconds it took to drag it and her cloak out from under the bed.

Her toes dug into cold mud and she let out a breath that she had not even known she was holding. *Safe. Almost safe.*

With a care not to slip in the mud, she made for the

shadows of the woods that lay near to Littlebury's village green and the Red Lion Inn. Silent now, she slipped behind the blacksmith's shop, and then into the woods. There, under the shelter of an oak, she stopped. Her lungs hurt from the cold air, but now she could afford to let out a deep sigh of relief.

Then, with her cloak still over her shoulders, she struggled into her dress, leaving the ties loose in back. As she straightened, a hand fell onto her shoulder.

Startled, she swung around, her fist clenched to strike, when a voice whispered with dry mockery, *"Droboy tume, Romale."*

THREE

The greeting, common enough among the Romany, eased open Glynis's fist. Relief warmed through her like the rush of good wine. *"Nais tuke,"* she whispered back, an edge to her thank you. Then she added, "For frightening ten years off my life. Why are you not waiting at the stream where we agreed to meet?"

She could not see his frown, but she knew it must be there on his handsome face. His dark coat—turned up to cover his white shirt—and dark breeches and soft, dark boots changed him into a towering shadow, rather like one of the oaks around them. As always, a sense of calmness came with him. But she knew—and could feel—the restless energy that lay under his surface composure. It was only when she saw Christo with his horses that she ever felt that the quiet of his body also filled his soul.

"You were late," he said, his voice soft but his words clipped. He had been worrying too much. He always did. "What went wrong? Wasn't it there?"

She shook her head and glanced back at the inn. Yellow candlelight spilled from the public room on the ground floor. The sound of a man's guffaw, and then the scrape of a fiddle being tuned, echoed in the night. From the upper story, Glynis glimpsed a chink of golden light as a curtain shifted. Her heart skipped a beat and a shiver chased across her bare arms.

"He had it, just as his servants said he would. But the story will have to wait. Come," she said, tugging on his coat sleeve for him to follow her into the woods.

He did not move.

With her eyes accustomed to the darkness, she stared up at him. The moon flirted again with the night, appearing from behind her veil of clouds, and gave light to the set of his clenched jaw and the impatience glinting in his eyes.

"Another time," she pleaded. "We knew this was a gamble, and we have lost. But there will be another time. A better time."

Wet leaves squelched as he shifted his weight. *Please, Christo,* she begged him silently. He had not her skills. Oh, he could charm easily enough, and could sell a blind horse to a crippled man. But too often he chose the straight path, no matter what its cost. And ever since they had learned the full truth of their inheritance, she had felt the frustration growing inside him. That lack of contentment had always been there, as it had with her. Now it had a channel inside him, and she had seen it start to change him.

He wanted—as did she—justice for what had been done to their father, to their mother, to them. But at times she feared that, in him, a dangerous need for revenge had started to grow.

Uneasy with such misgivings, she pushed them aside. They had troubles enough without allowing her inventive mind to see more than was there.

"Come," she said again, tugging on his arm, trying to pull him with her. They could not risk an open confrontation with Francis Dawes. As Lord Nevin, Dawes had power, and the law with him. To his kind, they were Gypsies. Vagrants. Thieves, liars, and outcasts. They had no land, no status, no rights. Dawes could have them arrested and transported for no more cause than his word that they had done wrong. He was a gentleman. *A lord,* she thought, with bitter scorn. And he had good reason to want them gone from this land. Or better still, to want them dead.

And who would question the death of a couple of Gypsies if a lord named them thieves?

Christopher had to know all of that. But would he allow caution to rule him—for this night, at least?

Reluctant, his steps dragging, he allowed her to turn him from the inn. A few steps later, they were at the stream, swollen from the spring rain. He lifted her over, and then jumped across the rushing water, his long legs easily clearing it, and his soft boots barely making a sound on the opposite bank.

Neither of them spoke as they slipped along the wooded path, back to where *Dej* and Bado waited for them.

Glynis tried to keep her thoughts on stepping over roots and ducking low branches, but her mind kept slipping back to that *gaujo*. It would be best if they traveled on tonight. She wanted miles between herself and the wicked Earl of St. Albans. But the uneasy feeling tickled along her spine like a spider dancing there that no matter where she went she would see him again.

Lord, how she hated things that were fated.

By dawn, St. Albans knew with a bone-deep resignation that he was going to be less than wise about this.

With a cooler head to rule him, he knew that he ought to allow the girl to slip away. Whatever mischief she was making was her own concern. She was, after all, a Gypsy, and therefore about as likely to behave herself as a feral cat. He had only his dislike of being made her dupe to drive him to hunt her.

Of course, there was also that too-tempting form of

hers, which had kept him restless and tossing last night. And she had shown sense as well as a clever mind—yes, a good deal of sense to run from him when she could.

However, she had set her will against his own.

And he simply could not allow her to do that.

Which meant that he would have to hunt her down. And the next time she turned her face up to him, it would not be with eyes shut tight and her mouth set, as if offering herself as a sacrifice. No, it would bloody well not be so. He wanted an image of her wanton and passionate, her body burning as his now simmered.

Blast her, but she had left him in an uncomfortable state, and that would have to be remedied. There was, after all, nothing that the Earl of St. Albans could not have if he so desired it.

But a voice inside mocked his thoughts with a sly, doubting memory of the things he had once wanted which had turned to dust when he had reached for them.

Oh, yes, you can have anything—anything that is made of vice and sin and earthly pleasure.

Quite stupidly, some small part of him still ached for those ghostly follies of his youth. He could recall being very young and inventing memories of the parents he had never known. This wistful longing was very like that.

His mouth twisted at such childish desires. Someday he really would find a way to destroy that last part of himself which still clung to this miserable nostalgic weakness. It really was a most uncommon nuisance to be plagued with that blasted emptiness. And he wondered with detachment if to obliterate that hole inside him might mean that he would have to destroy himself in the process. He rather suspected so.

Of course, he would be no great loss to the world, but it rankled him that his departure would cause a good deal of celebration in some parts of London. He did so hate to give his enemies any such satisfaction.

However, such gloomy thoughts did not become a spring morning, when birds sang like blissful idiots, and there was a pretty armful to find, with an amusing game of fox-and-hound to play.

With that in mind, he rose and summoned the landlord, in a better mood than he would have anticipated.

It took the better part of two hours to make himself presentable. He vowed a dozen times during that time never again to travel without his own servants. What had seemed in London a nuisance of an entourage following him now became a much desired necessity. He ignored his ruined blue coat, choosing instead a brown one from the light trunk he had had packed by his valet before he had left London a week ago. It took him six lengths of linen to tie a decent cravat, and he had to clench his back teeth to keep from muttering the oaths that filled his mind. But he would not lose his temper, despite being short of rest, badly dressed by his own exacting standards, and frustrated by his Gypsy's disappearance.

The only thing he could be grateful for was that the landlord's son had not cut him while shaving him.

At least, he thought as he sat down to a meal in the private parlor downstairs, the landlord set an excellent table. A pottery jug held ale—strong and dark. And upon the dark wood table sat a goodly sized beef haunch. Thick slices of ham lay upon a pewter plate, and hot bread that smelled of heaven had been carved into thick slices and left with a plate of fresh butter and a bowl of gooseberry jam. Simple fare, but it could almost make this forsaken hostelry reputable.

He ate well and spent his time leisurely gazing out the window to the village of Littlebury, bathed in mist, and thinking of his Gypsy.

It was all Gypsy stories that she had given him last night, he was certain of it. And yet . . . and yet . . . the curse of his own honesty thrummed in his chest like the shimmer of a bell that had been struck. He had learned the hard way how to detect a lie. And he had learned to beware those who used the illusion of virtue as a way to justify their sins. They were far more dangerous than any honest sinner.

But which parts of her story had been the truth, and what had been invention? She was very good at blending the two. Which meant that she had had a good deal of practice at it.

That thought roused a smile from him, and a stir of anticipation. What would she say when next he saw her? More lies? More tantalizing mixtures of truth and nonsense? He had no doubt that he would see her again. It mattered not where she hid. And it mattered even less if she were wed, for vows were made to be broken. It was why he avoided them.

Well, if she honestly did want something from Nevin, perhaps he would help her get it.

He frowned again.

Had that part been lies? It was possible that the robbery was no more than a way to cast herself into his path. He had certainly had other females attempt to gain his notice for their own purposes. An earl's coronet was a rather tempting prize, even if it came attached to a devil as black as he.

But, no, that did not feel right. He knew a few women capable of such twisted machinations, but he would wager the hundred guineas he had won at Newmarket that she had simply leapt to take advantage of opportunity.

What could she really want from Nevin? What really lay in that box, if there was such a box?

The jingle of harness and the stamping of horses in the yard roused St. Albans from the puzzle that his Gypsy had posed. Curious, he rose and went to the window.

A heavy black coach stood in the stable yard, a gold

crest upon the door, with seal bay horses being put into harness. Outriders in the somber dark blue of Lord Nevin's livery stood beside their mounts, talking idly with each other in the warming morning.

What ridiculous pomp. And altogether too tempting.

Putting on a pleasing smile, St. Albans sauntered outside to await Nevin's appearance.

He passed the time by critically surveying Nevin's team—too short in neck and too narrow, but flashy enough with their matched white stockings. He would not have given even one of them room in his stables.

Finally, Nevin came out of the inn, and St. Albans nodded a good morning to him.

The older man scowled, but St. Albans was far too accustomed to such black stares to take any notice.

"Did you ever find your Gypsy wench?" St. Albans asked, casually pulling out his snuffbox and speaking loud enough for grooms and servants to hear. As he expected, Nevin's face reddened at the innuendo that Nevin's reasons for wanting to find a Gypsy girl last night were far from proper. The man's self-righteous pride really was far too easy a target.

Nevin's mouth pulled down, accentuating the deep lines that bracketed his lips. "If you mean the thief who ransacked my rooms, I am certain she had aid in escaping justice. But I plan to lay a complaint with the magistrate before I quit the district. I am certain the law will not be kind to those who help such criminals."

Unmoved by this not-so-veiled threat, St. Albans selected a pinch of snuff and then asked, "Ransacked? Now there's a strong word. Tore your room apart, did she? Why, she must be a veritable Amazon. No wonder you were so anxious to find her."

Nevin's face darkened to the color of his burgundy coat. He really ought not to wear such a color, St. Albans thought, looking over the heavy coat with its gold brocade which would better suit the last century. Nevin was such a stick to abide by court dress that was more suited to the Queen's drawing room.

"You are insulting," Nevin growled, his fists clenched.

St. Albans allowed his stare to travel up and down the man's too-formal attire. The fellow prickled like a hedgehog, but something dangerous lay under that prickling as well. Something savage. It roused a like sensation in St. Albans.

Fixing a cold stare on Nevin, St. Albans drawled, "Always so satisfying to achieve a goal. Do you now feel compelled to call me out? If you do, I should mention that I never duel before noon. So tiresome to have to shoot a man before breakfast, but I thought we were speaking of you and your thief. What did she come for that you turn so prickly—the family jewels?"

Nevin's jaw worked, and St. Albans's smile widened into something almost genuine. There really was nothing better than to make oneself an irritation to those who were too smug in their delusions of righteousness.

For a moment, he really thought the man would turn away. Nevin was one of those who disdained dueling as barbaric—such nonsense, of course.

But the fellow hesitated, his chin still jutting forward, and a stubborn look in his eyes as if he could not let go of this, as if he had to make others see the truth of the matter as he saw it. "I have no idea what she could have wanted—other than whatever money or gems she might have found. That's the way of those Gypsies."

He spat the word out as if it were an unpleasant taste, and St. Albans had to check a spurt of anger. He took a breath, and took a rein on his temper, and then illumination clicked into place.

Good heavens, the man actually has something to hide. Fear had flickered at the back of his pale gray eyes.

And a touch of shame, for which he would probably rather die than admit.

St. Albans recognized the emotion at once. He always committed his sins in public, for it was impossible to carry shame for something the entire world knew. But what shame did Nevin hide?

Smiling, St. Albans flipped closed his snuff with his thumb and slipped the carved ivory box into his waistcoat pocket.

"I suppose those Gypsies look for whatever plump pocket is near. Yet, it is quite amazing that she went to your rooms, and did not bother with the guineas I left in mine. Do you think that mysterious Gypsy sense told her that you traveled with something far more valuable?"

Nevin's scowl deepened and he turned away, as if the conversation was over.

"It's Retribution," St. Albans said.

His expression startled, Nevin swung around to glare at St. Albans, that faint, shimmering fear back in those pale eyes.

How satisfying to score a point, St. Albans thought, now thoroughly enjoying himself. There seemed to be some truth to his Gypsy's story, after all.

"Retribution," he repeated. "The horse that won for me at Newmarket. Quite an amazing animal. By Aston, out of Forgetful."

Nevin's eyes blazed, and his mouth curved into something close to a snarl. St. Albans held still, waiting. How close to home had he struck?

Then, with his expression souring to disdain, Nevin's heavy chin lifted. "You're a damned wastrel, and a disgrace to your name."

"Oh, I waste nothing. I assure you of that."

Scowling, Nevin opened his mouth as if to say more, but a shout from one of the grooms drew his attention.

"Ready, m'lord."

With a last contemptuous glance at St. Albans, Nevin stalked away. His servants bowed before him, lowered the steps before he reached them, and then put them up again with a jumpiness that spoke of insecurity in their positions. Then, with coach horn blowing imperiously and outriders leading the procession, the heavy coach lumbered forward.

An impossible cavalcade to miss. And any fool—or Gypsy—could track and follow that parade. Well, that certainly made clear how his Gypsy came to take note of Lord Nevin. But just what had she come here to steal from the man?

It would take some work, unpleasant as that was, to discover the truth. However, he would console himself with the fact that his Gypsy would make it up to him someday.

Glynis watched her mother lay the cards upon the thick, gold Turkish carpet. Even though her mother could not see, she still knew the pattern of the cards. And she knew the cards by the feel of them, by the edges and nicks and the painted images on the old deck.

They sat on the ground, red pillows under her mother, but Glynis preferred the hard earth. She liked the connection to land, liked to feel the hum of it through her bones, and she loved the reassurance it gave her. The land would always be there. The seasons came in order. The world turned as it should. Those things she trusted. All else she regarded with deep suspicion.

Even the cards.

Too often they disappointed. In fact, all her life had seemed to be heartache after trouble. But it would not be like that forever. No. This year everything was changing. This year the wheel turned, and their lives would change. For the better—or for the worse.

She wanted that change, for the hope it brought that she might at last be able to have a real home. A cottage in a village was all that she had ever wanted. A place to live, where she was known and where she knew others. Christo wanted far more, but a house would be enough for her. A respectable house in a respectable village. And she wished for it with such a yearning that at times she feared it would never happen.

At those times her mother insisted on pulling out the cards, telling Glynis, "The card will show where trouble lays. When you know the path, it is easier to walk with courage."

I know where trouble lays, Glynis had thought, her mouth pulling down with annoyance. But she did not mention again the *gaujo* she had met.

It had been nearly a fortnight since her encounter with that *gaujo* and Francis Dawes. She had told Christopher and her mother only a sketch of what had happened: her attempt to steal the box, how she had hidden in the Earl of St. Albans's room, and how she had given up her clothes in order to slip away. Christo's expression had darkened at that, and Glynis had thought then that it would be a very good thing if he and that earl never chanced to meet.

Her mother had also frowned at the story, her sightless eyes clouded. Her mother still seemed a young woman, a little thickened by age, but still strong. Still vibrant. However, that day her face turned as gray as the streak that ran through the inky blackness of her hair, and for a moment, Glynis could only see the lines worn on her mother's narrow face. *Ah, she warned us not to act yet, and it did not go well.*

But her mother had only shaken her head, as if accepting an inevitable truth. Then she had turned away and had ordered Bado to pack the camp.

Having her mother say nothing—not even a rebuke

for ignoring her counsel—was far worse than any lecture. Glynis still cringed inwardly as she thought of the disappointment on her mother's face. She was such a bad daughter. But then she was bad at most things, except for her light fingers and her dancing.

Those talents seemed so little in this world.

Since then, they had traveled a good distance, stopping tonight outside the village of Epping. It was closer to London than Glynis recalled ever going before, and she knew that her mother—and Christo—were thinking of the great house in London. Lord Nevin's house, where Francis Dawes now lived.

However, it was not the proximity to him that had Glynis fussing with the campfire that night, making it and then remaking it three times before she had lit it. And it was not the warming, longer days, with a hint of summer in the night breeze, that left her restless. It was the thought that that *gaujo* might be near.

Shifting uncomfortably now, Glynis glanced around the small glade where they had stopped. Anything so that she did not have to look at the cards being laid down. She did not want to see what they might say. They might tell her too much truth.

Bado and Christopher had pitched the tents in the clearing of a stand of maples, and the trees were newly leafed in fresh green. Their pony—Kralisi—cropped grass nearby, her front legs hobbled, but 'Lisi never wandered far.

The two men had gone to a horse fair, and now Glynis wished she had gone with them. Only she might have been tempted into breaking her vow by liberating a few coins from some fat farmer's pockets.

Ah, well, soon Christo would be back with broken and ill-used horses that could be fattened on summer grass and retrained, and sold for a good profit. Bado knew how to whiten a horse's teeth and file them so that ten years looked like five. And Christo could teach a horse clever tricks that impressed a *gaujo* into paying more.

She wished she had such abilities, and not the curse of light fingers and a silent step. But her gift had sometimes been all that had kept them fed. She prayed now that her gift might be what could change the course of their lives.

With a quiet sigh, she glanced up to the sky, just turning purple at the top with the gathering night. *Someday,* she vowed to the first star she glimpsed, *someday I shall have a cottage with a cow and a garden, and then I shall never have to steal again. And I shall belong someplace. And Christo will—*

"You don't listen, *Chei!*"

Glynis straightened with a twinge of guilt. Her mother only used the Romany for *daughter* when she was irritated.

Running her touch over the ace of spades with a still-elegant hand, her mother said, "Preparation is needed. There is power to overcome obstacles, but only if you do not give in to bitterness. There is more at stake here than the material."

Wrinkling her nose, Glynis dutifully stared at the cards. It was like this always. With the cards, her mother saw things. She only saw cards. And only heard cryptic advice. Why couldn't the cards simply say, *Do this!* or *Do not do that!*

Her mother turned over the next card, laid it down, and read it with her touch.

"The king of spades," she said, her voice still clear and as strong as a young woman's, but her tone hushed. "The highest card, and yet this one can bring failure as well as success. He is the 'law," and yet his life is one of uncertainty in dealings with others. He is betrayed.

The choice is his to touch the world for good, or to sink to evil. Be cautious with this one. He will betray you."

Chewing on her lower lip, Glynis stared at the card. Who did the card stand for? For Francis Dawes? For that earl? For someone yet to come into her life? Someone in London?

Looking up, she stared into her mother's sightless gaze. "Who is he?"

Her *dej* began to gather the cards, and gave a small shrug. Her black shawl slid off the black of her dress. For as long as Glynis had memories, her mother had worn black. Even though she was young enough to have married again, she wore black for the dead husband she loved still.

"You will know," she told Glynis. "God gives you knowledge when you need it. Have patience for now."

With a frustrated growl, Glynis threw up her hands. "Patience. Whyever did you tell anything to Christo and I if we are only to sit on our hands and wait?"

"It was time to tell you."

"But not time to act! It never seems to be time to act."

Slowly, Glynis's mother climbed to her feet. Glynis rose as well, and then reached out to help her mother.

Swatting away Glynis's help, her mother straightened. "The time will come, as the time came to tell you. Bah! Christo at least listens. You! You are too like your father. You do not see that you cannot walk straight when the road is bent. And this road is very bent. Very bent. Beware the lesson your father had to learn."

Glynis swallowed the dryness in her mouth. Then her stare dropped. Her father had paid with his life for not listening.

She looked up to see her mother's dark form disappear into the nearest tent, the white canvas flap closing behind her.

Scuffing a stone with her boot, Glynis turned away from the tent and the firelight. She had not meant to be so disrespectful. But, oh, she did want to hurry this. She did not trust this waiting. She wanted this to be over. She wanted to know her place in this world. She wanted a home for her mother, and for Christo to be what he always should have been.

Perhaps she simply wanted too much.

Rubbing her arms against the cooling evening, Glynis walked to where 'Lisi grazed. She leaned her arm over the sturdy pony's back, not caring if white and black hairs and horse smells attached themselves to her dark blue dress. 'Lisi's warmth soaked into her, a comforting presence.

She had wished patience for Christo, but she ought to have included herself in that, too, it seemed. It had been as much her plan as his to give in to the temptation to do more than follow Lord Nevin's coach. And that had led them only to more disappointment. Ah, she should be used to that by now.

The steady sound of 'Lisi's grazing began to ease her unhappiness, but still that need to do something mixed uncomfortably with the dread that things really would not work out as she wanted. Ah, but she did not want to spend another winter in tents and on muddy roads. Her mother never complained, but Glynis hated it most when the icy weather came and her mother moved stiff and slow, like an old woman.

'Lisi shifted, moving to a new patch of grass. Glynis followed the pony, brushing shedding hair from the pony's back, scratching at the top of 'Lisi's shoulders.

"Ah, 'Lisi. Too bad I am not like you, and happy to be anywhere that thick grass grows."

'Lisi lifted her head and nodded, as if agreeing, but Glynis knew the pony was only enjoying the attention.

She smiled. And then the back of her neck began to tingle.

A branch snapped under a horse's step. Straightening, Glynis turned and started towards the sound, eager to see the horses Bado and Christo had bought. But it was a giant of a black horse that stepped from the shadows of the sheltering maples.

At the sight of the rider Glynis froze.

Him! That *gaujo!*

FOUR

For a moment, half-hidden by the shadowing trees, with his dark mount and his wicked beauty, he looked more like some lord of the fey folks rather than a mortal lord. His mount pawed the ground, restless, but he sat easily in the saddle. Everything came too easy to this one, Glynis thought, frowning at him.

His horse stepped forward and the last rays of daylight glinted in his hair. The breeze ruffled those deep bronze locks, disordering the curls into softness. His dark blue coat opened over a rich, gold brocade waistcoat, and the nipped waist made his shoulders look broader than she remembered. Only she knew that it was not padding that filled out his coat. She had seen the sleek muscles under his white shirt when she had stripped him.

The memory warmed her face, and she scowled at him. She would do best to remember that Lucifer, too, had the beauty of dawn in his face. And this devil was a *gaujo*. A Romany never came to any good at their hands.

Folding her arms, she deepened her scowl, hoping that would hide how her pulse quickened, and how sensations tingled upon her skin, and perhaps make him decide to turn and ride away again. If she had any sense, she would turn and run herself. But that had not gotten her very far from him, after all. And she had as much pride as he. So she braced her feet wider and narrowed her eyes.

This time, he was in her world. This time, he would be the one alone against her and her kind.

With a faint smile twisting his mouth, he swung off his black horse and left it standing, his reins dangling. She wished the animal would run off, but he had bewitched it as well, so that it stood patient and waiting, its black ears flickering towards its master.

Tucking a package wrapped in brown paper under his arm, the *gaujo* lord came towards her, lazy grace in every movement. As he neared, she saw the corner of his wide, sensual mouth lift a touch more, but wary caution lay in his green eyes.

Yes, you had better take care, my gaujo. I have more than one trick to play.

He stopped close enough to her that she could see the trace of golden beard on his cheek, and then her forehead tightened as she saw the faint, red line of a branch's slash across his left temple. Ah, but it was no concern of hers if he had so much conceit that he stayed mounted rather than walk on the ground like a Gypsy peasant when the branches thickened.

Oh, but why did she even notice such things?

He made her a bow as if she were a lady and they stood in the tame park of a great house, and then he held out the package to her. "I believe these are yours."

She glanced at the package, and then back at him. "You have nothing I want. Go home, *gaujo*. Before someone takes your pretty horse, or takes a dislike to your pretty face."

His smile widened to something warm and dangerously charming, and the green of his eyes deepened as wicked humor sparked there. She stiffened against that fascination he wove with so little effort.

"Pretty? You do say the most extraordinary things. I cannot recall anyone ever calling me pretty. Devilish, certainly. Remarkably good-looking has been mentioned by a few. Handsome is not often noted, but then handsome is as handsome does, and I so rarely do anything that is handsome by anyone."

His Gypsy stood there, glaring at him as if she wished she still had her hand wrapped around his pistol. And his fatigue, the disgust of the dust on his person, and displeasure with her for being so difficult to find—he had now lost his favorite hat to a low-slung branch—had vanished. He found a rare delight in how she always surprised him. And in how she took his breath away.

The setting sun cast golden light onto her skin, warming it as had the firelight the last time he had seen her. She wore a blue dress, high-waisted, but cut low and with a brightly patterned scarf tucked around her neck. He would have preferred to see her in less, but the dress nicely outlined the swell of her breasts and fell softly over the sweet curve of her hip.

With her dark hair pulled up into a careless knot, she made a tempting sight. He was glad now that he had pushed on, forging a path through that impossible bramble of woods.

"Come, where is your curiosity?" he asked, determined to lure her into conversation. "If not about the package, then why not ask how I found you?"

She lifted one shoulder, and he thought how delicious that movement would be if she wore nothing at all. Her sharp voice brought him back to the moment. "Why should I ask? So you may brag, and show how clever you are? Well, how clever is it to find your way and lose your hat?"

Stung by her comment, his lips thinned as he pressed them tight. It was not so much the reminder of his lost hat that bothered him. It was that she had just laid bare the exact reason why he had wanted her to ask—he had wanted her to think him clever. He had wanted it enough, in fact, that he had taken this hunt quite personally, rather than sending someone to simply fetch her to him. He had wanted her to see just what he could do.

Unaccustomed to having anyone see through to his motives so well, he was not certain he cared for it. It left him feeling curiously . . . well, not quite vulnerable, but certainly far more exposed than he liked.

For a moment, he toyed with giving in to the impulse to simply do what he wished, which was to drop his package and drag her into his arms. It would serve her well for pulling a tiger's tail. But he had ridden miles, following nearly impossible Gypsy signs left in branches and rock for other Gypsies, and had paid an extravagant sum for such knowledge from others of her vagabond tribe. He had had his servants seeking information of her that he could follow. He was hungry, tired, and he had spent the last two restless weeks dreaming of a proper seduction.

And she was not, he thought firmly, going to pull this out of his control by rousing his temper. This game required expert finesse, not brute strength which any oaf could muster.

Besides, he had gone to all this effort because she had seemed to be an original. He ought to be pleased that she was that—and much more.

So he smiled and said, "Very well, I won't tell you." *At least not until you beg it of me.* "Now, do you want your package, or shall I just take it with me and depart? I should mention, however, that there is more here than you expect. I am at least a clever enough fellow to know when I owe a lady an apology."

Her eyebrows arched with surprise, but her dark eyes remained wary as a cornered vixen's. However, he knew when he had caught a woman's interest. Gypsy or lady, what woman could resist the lure of respect? That trick always worked far better than any diamonds.

He pushed the package towards her again. "It is getting rather heavy for me to continue holding out in this conciliatory fashion."

She stared at him a moment longer, as if she half-expected him to jump upon her. An enticing image, but he had far more interesting plans for her.

Gingerly, she took the package. She was careful not to touch his hand, he noted. An excellent sign, for it meant that his touch could affect her in ways she must guard against. Oh, he was going to enjoy teasing her out from behind her wise caution.

As she untied the twine, she bit her lower lip, and the gesture shot a jolt of lust through him, just as it had the last time he had seen her do that.

His skin warmed, and he thought with delight that she was going to be worth losing a dozen hats for.

The twine fell loose, the paper parted, and she gazed down at the neatly folded silk chemise, the new corset he had purchased for her, and on top of them the mate to his own silver filigree pocket pistol.

"I thought that if you planned to continue your career as an adventuress, you might wish to do so properly equipped. The pistol is not loaded—I am also clever enough not to tempt you, you see. But I will show you how to care for it later, if you wish."

With one hand supporting the package, she reached up to slide her fingers over the pistol and then over the silk, her touch reverent as if she had never seen such things.

St. Albans stepped closer with the intent of explaining a few features of the pistol, and of also placing himself in a better position to accept her gratitude. His focus centered on her. On how she had drawn in a deep breath that swelled her chest. On how her eyes darkened with delight. On the hint of a smile now curving her lips. He took a certain satisfaction in being able to read a lady so well, and he knew this one to be pleased. And a little confused by her own feelings.

It would take only a little encouragement now to assist her in resolving those feelings into something mutually delightful.

But just as he started to lean closer to her, something sharp pricked the middle of his back, stopping him more effectively than did the low voice that growled, "Another step and you die, *gaujo!*"

Anger blazed for an instant inside him. His muscles tightened. No one threatened the Earl of St. Albans. And he had had about enough interruptions of his Gypsy's seduction. If he had another coat ruined over this Gypsy girl, someone would pay dearly for it.

He forced his body to relax into deceptive ease, and his temper to cool, and then he began to shift his weight so that he could kick back and snag the other man's feet out from under him. He wanted his hands around this imbecile's throat.

A soft touch on his arm stopped him.

Glancing down, intent tangled with anger at the sight of his Gypsy's face turned up to his and silently begging him to be still. Oh, blazes, but she was an inconvenience just now. He did not want to be distracted, yet here she was, making it difficult for him to even think, let alone act.

He still ached to throttle the dolt who had dared threaten him, but it seemed that his Gypsy had other plans.

Glancing over his shoulder, she spoke rapidly in that odd language of her kind to the man with the knife. And it occurred to St. Albans that she was actually defending him.

He stared at her, astonished. No one shielded the Earl of St. Albans. Or at least no one had ever thought such a thing might be necessary. Not even among the all-too-numerous uncles and aunts who had raised him could he conjure such a memory. Oh, they had leapt readily enough to his command. He had learned early, after all, just how much power an earl wielded. But defend him? That was absurd.

However, here she was, hotly arguing with one of her kind on his behalf.

For a moment, he wondered if he ought to feel affronted that she thought such effort necessary. But he was having the worst time coming up with any feeling just now other than a deep desire to touch his lips to the curve of that determined jaw of hers. And a wry amusement.

Would this not astonish half of London—and leave the other half laughing—to think that a Gypsy had defended the notorious Earl of St. Albans.

Easing his shoulders, he began to enjoy the situation—and the view. His Gypsy's eyes glittered, color blazed on her cheekbones, and that chin of hers lifted with determination. He would simply have to indulge her, if for no other reason than to see what happened next.

The idiot she argued with had been making his own intentions quite clear, and the pressure of a blade dug deeper, causing St. Albans to wince. *Another coat ruined,* he thought, deeply irritated as the warmth of blood trickled down his spine. Well, no matter. The fellow would pay later. In kind.

Another jab and St. Albans's temper flared again. That did it. His Gypsy might be a tempting morsel, but she was doing a poor job as his champion, and he was really not going to allow himself to be skewered simply to indulge her.

Just as he braced for action, a sharp voice cut through the gathering twilight, stopping everything.

"Chavaia!"

Despite the odd language, the command to stop came

across as plain as if it were the King's English. St. Albans focused his attention on the woman who commanded so much respect here.

Dressed in black and with the twilight gathering close, he thought at first that she must be an old Gypsy woman. Silver streaked her hair in a dramatic bolt that added to his first impression, and she felt her steps with a cane. However, as she came closer, he noted the straight figure, age-thickened, yes, but not too bent by time. And while her weathered face made it difficult to place her exact years, he doubted if she had reached a half a century yet. A black shawl lay loose over her black dress, but he noted her garments only with a casual glance. Her presence demanded far more of his attention.

She had black eyes, unfocused, but with an assessing intelligence glittering there, and sharp cheekbones, nose, and jaw, which showed a great beauty that was maturing into magnificent ruins. Despite her small stature, she certainly knew how to wield power. He always admired strength.

The annoying sting at his back vanished, and St. Albans found himself facing this woman.

He started to look for where his Gypsy girl had gone, but the woman captured his face between her hands. He began to pull away, resenting and resisting such intimacy, but the Gypsy held tight.

Putting up his own hands, he took her wrists to pull away those roughly callused hands of hers. He did not like to be touched. Never had. Oh, he could enjoy a woman's body well enough, but that was an entirely different thing from having this . . . this familiarity pushed upon him.

However, the woman would not let go, and he would look a fool to struggle with her.

So he dropped his own hands and stared back at her, one eyebrow lifted, waiting and wishing for her to finish her nonsense. Some rubbishing Gypsy superstition, no doubt.

It took an effort not to grow restless under that blank and empty black-eyed gaze. And then her fingers began to roam over his face. He fought down the uneasy feelings that began to stir inside him, the sense that she honestly was seeing more than he cared to reveal. The urge to fling off her hands grew stronger, almost overruling his control. He clenched his back teeth and vowed that this woman would not stare him down.

And then it struck him.

Devil a bit, but she was blind. That was why her stare slid through him, and why she used her touch as her eyes. He relaxed, deciding that he would permit this liberty with his person, for even he had his limits of detestable behavior, and rudeness to blind women certainly lay beyond his depths of depravity.

Finally, she let him go, and he had the most peculiar reaction.

Regret.

The feeling washed over him along with the cold air that bathed his face where her warm hands had but a moment ago held him still. Curiously, he could not understand this . . . this sense of loss. As if the part of him that had always been empty had been briefly filled, and now lay . . .

But what utter rot! This Gypsy had a bewitching trick to her, and that was all. He was not about to become like his Aunt Julia and give in to a belief in mystic nonsense.

He blinked away his disoriented feelings, dismissing them. These Gypsies dealt in the pretense of such special powers, of living in the unseen. He would do well to remember that.

The older woman stepped back, sliding her cane from under her arm where she had tucked it, and then surprised him again with a voice that would have suited a Mayfair drawing room. "He will stay. Bado, see to his horse. Christo, put away your *tshuri*. Come, daughter, we have a guest for dinner."

St. Albans glanced behind him and locked stares with a younger man. Dark-haired like all the Gypsies, tall and well-muscled, the fellow had an arrogant face and an insolent manner. There was enough resemblance to his Gypsy to make St. Albans wonder if the fellow was a relative. He certainly hoped so, for he really did not want to deal with a jealous lover. That was such a predictable nuisance.

Slipping his snuffbox from his waistcoat pocket, St. Albans watched the fellow sheath his knife—the *tshuri* that the older woman had mentioned, no doubt. Then he allowed his gaze to travel over the Gypsy's worn coat, down to his patched breeches and dusty boots, and back up to the fellow's face.

St. Albans gave him a cold smile. "Do be a good fellow and give Cinder some oats if you have any."

The Gypsy's jaw tightened, and for an instant St. Albans thought the fellow would be reckless enough to come after him now. *Oh, please do,* St. Albans thought, his dislike for the fellow growing stronger.

But then the younger man's shoulders relaxed and he flashed a contemptuous grin, and spoke, his accent as unexpectedly well bred as the old woman's. "I suppose a man who cannot even look after his own horse has to rely on others to do for him. Don't worry, *gaujo*. Tonight you are a guest. But tonight is only tonight."

Turning, the young Gypsy walked away, taking with him his companion, an older man, also dark-haired, but short, stout, and balding, with a wicked scar down his cheek. St. Albans watched as they tended to his own mount, and to the three bony, disreputable-looking horses they had led into the clearing.

Insolent pup, St. Albans thought, irritated with the Gypsy. And then he dismissed the fellow. It would be a different matter, of course, if the fellow were a gentleman and offered such an insult. But he was only a Gypsy, after all, and far below the notice of the Earl of St. Albans.

The Gypsy girl, however, was a different matter.

Turning, he strode towards the campfire, where the Gypsy women were busy setting up a cooking pot over the open flame and busying themselves with a rabbit to skin—poached in a snare, no doubt. And arguing in their own language.

He could not follow the words, but from the tone of it, he could guess that it was not a question of how much salt to add. No, he was quite certain they were talking about him.

Why had the older woman decided that he could stay?

"Why did you ask him to stay?" Glynis muttered to her mother, speaking in Romany. "He will only make problems."

She cast a glance from the corner of her eye at St. Albans, who had stretched his tall, lean frame out beside the fire, lounging on the golden carpet as if he lay in the woods every night.

Her mother gave a shrug that could mean anything. "Yes, this one is good at making problems. But it is problems that we also seek to make, daughter."

"You are the one always urging caution—patience."

Anna smiled at her daughter. She had so much to learn, yet. For a moment, the worry came back. Had she shielded them too much? Should she have told them the truth sooner? But when? When could she have told them? When they were children and their lives were in danger? No, fate had woven the pattern. She had taught them caution, and kept the truth to herself, because it had been the only path at the time.

But this *gaujo* lord brought new paths. She could feel them stirring. Her Glynis was right to be cautious. But too much caution now could be as fatal as too much daring. They walked a rope over a chasm now. And the only way to walk on a rope was to look ahead—not down at fears, or backwards to the past.

So Anna put away her fears and her unspoken regrets, smiled at her daughter again, and put her to work cutting the carrots and potatoes bought from the village market yesterday.

"An excellent meal," St. Albans said. He lay back so that he was propped up on one elbow. He had been on alfresco picnics that were far less enjoyable than this. The firelight warmed his face, and while a slight chill lay on his back, the wine heated him from within. That and watching his Gypsy girl—Glynis, the older woman had called her.

No one had asked for his name, so he assumed they knew it. He was accustomed to having his reputation precede him, just not in these unlikely circles.

In truth, the meal had been quite good. The blind Gypsy woman managed to bake bread in a pot—heavens knew how. The stew, if not a delicacy, at least provided decent fare. And they finished with apples—stolen, St. Albans suspected, but ripe—a sharp Stilton cheese, nuts, and a strong but drinkable red wine.

Of course, conversation had been somewhat lacking.

The older man—Bado, he seemed to be called—sat beside the younger Gypsy, his covetous stare focused on Cinder, who grazed contentedly beside the Gypsy horses. The younger fellow—Christo—glared at St. Albans and said nothing.

The older woman seemed content to say little, and his

Gypsy, Glynis, glowered at him as if this situation was all of his making.

So he did his best to amuse himself.

He told them how he had paid a fellow to learn their Gypsy signs. His Glynis exchanged an uneasy glance with the one called Christo, who shrugged back an answer, and St. Albans wondered just what relation these two had to each other that they could speak without words. A close one, he thought, disliking the young Gypsy fellow even more.

His story wound down, and then there was nothing but the crackle of young wood on fire. The scent of stew and smoke hung in the clearing, a gamy, sharp, pleasant smell. The wine danced nicely in St. Albans's head.

He did not want to leave—mostly because that young Gypsy idiot seemed to be wishing him on his way. But also because he had not hit upon a plan to pull his Gypsy girl away from the protection of her kind and more firmly into his reach.

Unfortunately, she seemed quite close with the older woman—her mother, he decided, after studying the similarities in face and form.

With all the freedom she seemed to enjoy, she would have no wish to rebel. So she could not be tempted into defying her elders. But he needed her indebted to him. Gratitude was always such a useful emotion in a seduction. And he wanted her in a setting that was more conducive to intimate relations.

Pleasant as this spring night was, he was also starting to get a crick in his back, and he had never been fond of moonlit forests for trysts. Far too many insects, animals, and scratching thorns.

Well, there was but one way to gain knowledge.

Smiling, he sipped his wine from the pottery cup provided to him. Then he asked, "I take it that you travel to London? Still after Nevin, are you?"

Glynis scowled at him. She had been poking at the fire with a stick, and now her hand stilled. She glanced at Christo, who looked as unhappy as she at this question.

Ah, this *gaujo* lord, this St. Albans, knew too much about them. What if, in London, he talked to others about their interests? And what if such talk got back to Francis Dawes?

That could ruin everything.

Turning slightly, she covered her mother's hand, her grip tight, asking the silent question—*what do we tell him?*

Her mother sat very still. Firelight danced over her face, making familiar features seem mysterious. For a moment, Glynis glimpsed the young woman who had broken so many men's hearts before she gave her own— once and forever.

Slowly, her mother nodded, as if coming to an important decision, and then she said in Romany, "It is in water that one learns to swim. It is started. Answer him. And let us see where fate takes us next."

Beside her, Glynis felt Christopher stiffen, and then he answered back in Romany, his words hot and low, "What if this *gaujo* talks to others? He asks too many questions."

Glynis shifted her touch to Christo's arm. "Then let us answer some so that he stops asking."

"Why? He has no reason to help us. And what if he is a friend to Lord Nevin?"

He spat out the last words, and his hate left Glynis frowning. He was not seeing clearly because his feelings blinded him, she knew.

She glanced across the flames to the earl. She trusted him no more than she trusted any *gaujo*—and yet . . . ah, something inside her whispered that she could. She did not want to listen to that voice. What if it was only desire talking? What if that voice was a wish that held as much substance as the smoke from the fire?

And then, staring across the flickering flames at his handsome face, at his fine clothes and those wicked green eyes, she thought of Christo's words, and she remembered how little love this *gaujo* had had in his voice when he had spoken to Francis Dawes.

It flashed into her mind that perhaps they shared a common dislike. And he had offered, had he not, that perhaps he would help her get what she wanted.

She also had something this *gaujo* wanted—herself. Could she dance with the devil and not get burned?

Excitement began to stir inside her as plans took shape.

Looking at Christo, Glynis asked in Romany, her voice shaking a little from the daring of her ideas. "This one, he goes where he pleases in London. We cannot do that."

Christo shot a dark look at the *gaujo*. "And what do you think his help will cost you?"

Glynis's chin went up. "Only as much as I am willing to pay. Remember that. I have a right to my own choices, too."

Frowning, Christo thought this over. His expression did not lighten, but at last he nodded. "You do. As I make mine."

Glynis nodded, not very satisfied with his answer, but she doubted she would get any enthusiastic agreement from him for what she was now thinking.

She glanced back to St. Albans and found him staring at her, his eyes narrowed and his mouth twisted. He looked hard and dangerous, and Glynis's certainty that she could handle him faltered.

Sitting up, he said, his voice careless, but with a sarcastic tone underneath the drawl, "Do you know, I had no idea a few simple questions could stir up such controversy. Are you discussing my poor choice of topics, or whether he should slit my throat now or later? So tedious of me, I know, not to have a better grasp of the Gypsy tongue, but then my education was sadly restricted to French, Italian, German, Greek, and a smattering of Latin that never took."

Glynis almost smiled with relief. He was insulted, that was all. Typical of a lord. He did not like being shut out by their discussion. Ah, but it had been rude of them to speak of him as if he were a thing, not a person.

"I am sorry," she said, her face hot, and not just from the fire. "We are not accustomed to guests, and so you shall have to consider that it is only that we feel as comfortable as if you were one of our own."

His mobile face shifted, the left eyebrow lifting with skepticism. She had overdone her apology, offering too much flattery, so she shifted her tone to one more matter-of-fact. "But you had asked of Lord Nevin—and if we go to London."

"I had," he said, his voice neutral.

"You must know that we do. We have to. You see, Francis Dawes—the man you call Lord Nevin—he is my uncle, and he stole my inheritance."

FIVE

St. Albans almost laughed.

Here she was—gaze steady, hands still in her lap, not so much as a quiver of her lip or a flicker of discomfort—giving him yet another *swato*. First mistress, then married, now a niece. Still, he liked this tale better than the others. It even seemed plausible.

In truth, he could almost picture Nevin refusing to acknowledge such a low relation as a Gypsy niece, even one born on the wrong side of the blanket. The man's insufferable pride was renowned. But had there been a brother—elder or younger?

Dredging through memory, St. Albans could not recall enough of the Dawes family, but it would be the matter of a moment to verify the lineage. She must know that. But the rest of her story seemed as difficult to prove a lie as it would be to prove the truth.

Interested, despite that he knew better than to be taken in by such tales, he said, "And may I ask, without engendering another long discussion in your native tongue, how do you plan to gain what is owed you?"

Her stare dropped for a moment, so that she gazed into the dancing yellow flames. He had the feeling she was weighing what else to tell him.

Then she admitted, "I did not lie about that box. There is one and it holds papers that could prove my claim."

"And so you plan to . . . ?" St. Albans let his words

trail off. He had been about to ask if she thought, once she had these papers, to take Nevin to court. It would certainly take that—and more—to pry anything loose from Nevin's hands.

However, that assumed there honestly were papers hidden in some box, as well as a box to steal. For all he knew, she had made up this entire story from smoke and starlight. Only one thing stood quite clear—she was withholding something. He could sense that.

Which meant that he would have to dig further, and it annoyed him more than a little that he actually wanted to know the whole story.

Well, since his Gypsy certainly seemed to act only on opportunity—while he was cursed with a mind that constantly saw around corners—he began to calculate those corners for her. And the more he turned over the schemes in his mind, the better he liked them.

He swirled his wine in its cup. "Do you know, I actually might be able to offer some assistance."

The young Gypsy gave a rude snort, but Glynis glared at the fellow, and then glanced back at St. Albans, her expression guarded. "Why would you want to help us?"

"Why not? It is no matter to me what trouble you plan for Nevin, and it would be amusing to be at hand to see the mischief. But I would ask for something in return."

Her dark eyebrows lifted. "What would you ask?"

St. Albans smiled. "Your company in London while you are there as my mistress."

Everyone seemed to be on their feet at once. Knives hissed from their scabbards and flashed in the firelight. The sudden movement startled the horses, and St. Albans felt their hooves thud against the ground as their nickers stirred the air.

He remained stretched out on the carpet, his pottery mug of wine in hand, looking up with mild interest at the faces that glowered over him. It seemed these Gypsies were quite protective of their women. Well, now that he had shocked them thoroughly, he could make his offer into something that seemed reasonable, and more acceptable.

St. Albans glanced back to Glynis, who stood next to the younger Gypsy fellow, a restraining hand on his arm. "Really now, I could hardly pass you off as anything except a mistress. The ladies I take up with are too soon ladies no longer. But the pose would guarantee you proximity. Nevin may be high in the instep, but he has the normal vices, and he moves in the same world I occupy."

Her mouth pulled down and her chin lifted. "I am not interested in being any man's mistress!"

With a shrug, he put down his mug. "That, my dear, would be your choice. I am simply offering you access."

He spread his own hands wide, palms up, and offered one of his more innocent smiles. And if he could not seduce her into doing more than posing as his mistress, then he did not deserve to be called the worst scoundrel in London.

The young Gypsy, Christo, started to say something in his language, his tone low and fierce, but his meaning quite clear. He was not the trusting sort. The older woman silenced him with a word, and then frowned. She wasn't the trusting sort either, it seemed.

St. Albans focused his attention on his Gypsy—his Glynis.

She stepped around the fire, coming to his side and he rose as she did so. She stared at him so intently that for a moment he thought she would take his face in her hands as had her mother. But she simply glared at him, her eyebrows flattened over her dark eyes, her chin lowered, her tempting mouth in a set line.

Turning, she said something in her Gypsy tongue to her mother, who nodded to the older Gypsy man. He vanished into the darkness, and when he came back, he gave something to his Gypsy. Cards, St. Albans noted with a touch of surprise. Did his Gypsy intend to let luck decide? Devil a bit, but she was a reckless one.

His Gypsy took the cards and split the deck to shuffle the worn cards by sliding part of the pack into the rest. Then she fanned out the faded, painted backs. Firelight glimmered on the worn deck.

"Take one," she said.

He did. And then turned it over.

The king of spades. Well, it was a high card at least. Was it high enough? Would she draw a card now?

He glanced down at his Gypsy. Her eyes had gone wide, and one hand had come up to her chest.

What? Did that mean a good omen, or bad? Blazes, but he could almost wish she would decide with her heart, or her head, or her instincts, but not with this nonsense. Nothing guided him but his own will. And the same was true for her.

Why in Hades was he spending so much effort on her? She was but a woman, like any other. And he had spent far too much time on her as it was.

He glared down at her, unreasonably displeased that she could not give him a simple yes or no.

"My coach will be at the crossroad to Chelmsford. Tomorrow at sunset. If you want proximity to Nevin, I can give you that. But make your choice soon."

With a curt nod, he turned on his heel and strode toward his horse. The point between his shoulders where the knife had dug in earlier ached with each step, further irritating him.

Would she come on the morrow? Or would she run shy again? And what had she seen in that card that had made her face pale in the firelight?

He glanced down at his hand, saw the card still there and almost flung it away. Then he changed his mind. He would return it to her when next they met. Only it was not fate that they would meet again. It was his own desire.

Gathering up Cinder's reins, he swung up on the black horse without bothering with the stirrups. Then he glanced back.

His Gypsy still stood beside the fire, and the air around her crackled from tension, as if a storm had gathered in the night.

No one said anything as he rode away.

Well, the lot of them would learn soon enough that what the Earl of St. Albans wanted, he got. By whatever means necessary.

Glynis stood at the edge of the woods, a change of clothing and a few necessities wrapped in a bundle that weighed heavy on her arms. A breeze, cool with evening air, brushed her face, tugged loose a strand of her hair, and brought the dusty smell of roads.

At the crossroad between Epping and Chelmsford, a black coach waited beside the dusty road. A coachman perched on his seat and two footmen stood at the back wheels.

Glynis wet her parched lips. Her heart beat faster than it should after the walk here, and her courage was leaking out of her like sand from a tight fist.

She had parted from Christo with an argument, and those hot words sat badly with her. No matter that Bado had only shrugged his lack of any opinion, or that her *dej* had said with a frown that the cards had spoken and what would be would be. Christo had voiced everyone's misgivings—even her own.

This earl would take her, use her as he wished, and abandon her. How could she trust a *gaujo,* after all? He could do with her as he willed once she stepped into his coach.

Glynis's anger had roused at that point. "I am three years older than you," she had flashed back at Christo. "And I am not some simpering lady who cannot cross a puddle without getting wet! This is a chance we cannot ignore."

At that, Christo had stormed off, cursing her foolish stubbornness. But Glynis had made her decision.

It was a risk. But so was picking coins out of a man's pocket. As always, her needs—all their needs—were far stronger than any worries.

She also knew in her bones that that *gaujo* had meant what he had said. It would be her choice to become mistress in more than appearance. Yes, he wanted her—but she had seen also that he wanted to prove he could make her want him. Well, let him try.

But still the words of the maids at the inn echoed in her mind—this was a man who could make any woman love him. And what if that were true?

She tightened her grip on her bundle, feeling the cloth bunch under her fingers.

If this earl was even half of what the maids had whispered, he was far too dangerous for her tastes. Such a man would take her heart, and leave her with only memories and an empty bed, and an ache where once he had lived.

As her mother had been left.

So she would be careful as she danced with this devil. She would get what she wanted and find a way to keep him distant, from her heart if from nothing else. She had the warning of the card, after all. And she had her mother's example of twenty years alone.

Drawing a deep breath, Glynis started towards the Earl of St. Albans's coach, with its crest upon the door and its four black horses whose gleaming coats glinted blue in the dying sunlight.

The coach door stood open, the steps down, and as she neared he stepped out onto the dusty road.

He looked far more like a lord, with a tall hat set at a rakish angle, a beautiful brown coat molded to his broad shoulders, buff breeches, and boots that shone like black mirrors. Almost, she could imagine him a stranger.

Then a familiar smile crooked the right corner of his mouth. "I knew you had courage enough. You are indeed a remarkable woman, Glynis Dawes."

She wrinkled her nose. "I use my mother's name— Chatwin."

St. Albans swept off his hat and bowed. "Then, Miss Chatwin, your carriage awaits." And because she looked up at him, her eyes enormous and her cheeks pale under her golden skin, he found sympathy enough for her that he gave her a rueful smile. "Don't tell me you have any fear of a man you've already seen naked?"

Her glance sharpened. "I left before you had your trousers off," she said, and then she peered into the carriage as if it were a cell in London's White Tower.

Oh, for . . . St. Albans thought, his patience snapping.

Sweeping his arms around her, he pinned her own arms tight to her side, pulling her soft curves against him. The bundle she carried wedged between them, but he disregarded it. She struggled only a moment, only until she realized it was of no use, and then, stiff with outrage, she turned angry dark eyes up to him.

He smiled down at her. "Yes, I am stronger than you, and I could easily force my will on you."

And for a moment it was almost too tempting to do just that. He burned for her. He wanted to kiss her until her resistance melted and her resolve fled. He had waited too long for her already.

But she had raised the stakes for him last night, and now it would not be enough simply to have her.

He wanted her willing and desperate with longing. He wanted her aching with need. He wanted her on his terms.

He knew a thousand ways to seduce a woman. One of them would work with her. She had set her will against his, and had set him a challenge to break her with fair means and foul, so that she was the one who gave in.

Releasing her, he smoothed the arms of her gown, swept her cloak back to cover her shoulder from where it had fallen away. Then he lifted her chin with one gloved finger.

"There now, the worst that could happen has not. So there's no need to cower in a corner of my carriage."

She lifted her chin from his touch, and gave him a cool stare. "I never cower. And I have your pistol with me—loaded now. And if you had not let me go, I would have shot you in the foot, and that, I think, would have dampened your ardor. Now, do you help me into the coach, or does your mistress have to fend for herself?"

For a moment, he did not believe her. Glancing down, he saw that she had indeed slipped a hand into the bundle she carried. It had not been a bluff. She had been ready to shoot him if need be.

He smiled, delighted. She was going to be more than a challenge. She might actually be his greatest conquest.

With a bow, he handed her into the coach and climbed up after her. The footmen put up the steps and closed the doors as he settled himself in the corner opposite her, his legs stretched diagonally across the carriage so that his boots brushed her skirts and touched her ankles.

"How do you care to pass the hour or so that it will take us to reach London? Cards, perhaps?" He pulled the king of spades from his pocket.

She reached for it, but he held it away.

"I take it it's a good card?" he asked, staring at the dark king's painted image. Then he glanced at her.

She gave a small shrug. "What is good for one person can mean harm to another."

His mouth twisted. "I suppose it could. Does that mean you do not believe in evil, only in the harm caused by someone else's good?"

"No. There is evil. And perhaps the worst evil is when harm is done under the pretense of good."

Her words came out tinged by bitterness, and he wondered if that was a barb meant for him, or someone else. "That is certainly the worst hypocrisy . . . but are there not seven deadly sins? Are those not evils as well?"

Again, she shrugged and turned to look out the window, although there was little enough to see in the dusk of twilight.

Give her time, he warned himself. *Go slow. These affairs are always over too fast as it is.*

Tipping his hat down over his eyes, he crossed his arms and settled himself against the carriage squabs. "Well, we all look after our own interests. As I intend to do now. You will forgive me, my dear. Rest yourself, if you can."

He relaxed, but he listened to her breathing as he pretended to sleep. Truth was, however, that he was fatigued. He had ridden to London last night, for he'd had arrangements to make, and then he had paced his room until dawn, wondering if she would meet him or not. He could not recall the last time he had expended such energy for a woman. Had he ever done so? Once perhaps, when he was young and still had dreams. But why exert himself so much now?

Pondering that, his mind began to drift, and his last conscious thought was a surprising realization that it had been a feeling of relief that had swept over him when he had seen her step from the woods.

Then his breaths slowed and deepened, and he fell asleep.

From her corner of the coach, Glynis stared at the Earl, with his tall beaver hat pulled low over his eyes and his shoulders relaxed against the plush velvet of the seat, and his chest rising and falling in even, slow measures.

Either he had no conscience at all, or he had a cat's ability to sleep when he pleased. Yes, that would suit him.

Leaning forward, she glanced outside the coach's glass window, ignoring the luxury around her of velvet and drapes and such comfort as she had never known. She could not enjoy it, not with her nerves tight and her fists clenched around her bundle.

The world had darkened to shadows, but she thought she glimpsed a rider, following at a distance. She hoped so. Her arms still burned from where this *gaujo* had held her tight, and her skin still tingled. And she was not certain that, had he really kissed her, she would have shot him.

She glanced back to the Earl. He did not seem so bad like this, with that mouth of his softened, and without its usual twist. What had put that scorn in his smile, and did he think only of himself because he had never had anyone else to think about?

Uncomfortable with this image of him—not as an earl, or as a *gaujo,* but just as a man—she turned her stare back to the window and the darkness outside.

St. Albans woke to the clatter of iron horseshoes on pavement. That meant that the London road had been left behind and the carriage had gained the paved streets of Mayfair. Sitting up, he pulled off his hat and raked a hand through his hair, and then he caught a glimpse of Glynis as the carriage passed near the flambeaus that illuminated one of the great houses.

She lay curled up on the seat opposite, her head pillowed on one arm, her feet tucked under her skirts. Her dark cloak spilled off her shoulder and one hand lay in nerveless relaxation over her slim, cloth bundle.

Watching her, he realized that he had never before watched anyone sleep. The women he had bedded, he never slept with. Pleasure was pleasure, and for rest he sought his own solitary bed, as he had all his life.

But it was rather pleasant to watch her now, her face relaxed and unguarded, one hand curled close to her chin, her chest rising and falling with slow, deep breaths. She frowned in her dreams, her brow tightened, and she hunched a shoulder, as if to shake off some trouble.

What is it you really want, my Gypsy? Will you ever tell me?

Only he could not imagine why she would ever tell him anything, other than another of her stories. He was the enemy. A dreaded *gaujo*. And she was a wild Gypsy who lied and stole and schemed.

For some reason that image sat badly with him tonight. She did not look a Gypsy just now. She looked a lady with troubled dreams. A lady in need of shelter and strong arms about her. A lady who . . .

His mouth twisted. Such nonsense. Despite her lovely voice, she was no lady. She was a Gypsy. She had been ready to shoot him earlier if he presumed too much. As she would probably shoot him now if he sought to press his advantage. He really ought to confine his imaginings to his own concerns, only she was his concern now. He wanted her happy, for that would make her compliant.

What did his Gypsy want of Nevin?

The carriage rocked to a halt. St. Albans glanced out,

and when he looked back, his Gypsy had stirred and now sat up, rubbing the sleep from her eyes, her expression cross.

Then she sat bolt upright. "London! And I missed seeing it?"

She sounded so upset that he had to smile. "It's dark already, with little enough to see. I shall take you driving tomorrow, and you may look your fill in the daylight."

"But I wanted to see it from afar. And the city gates. Are there really hundreds of chimneys?"

"Thousands, I expect. Do you wish me to hire you a balloon, so that you could sail over them in the air?"

Frowning, she shook her head. "A balloon? No. I saw one of those once in the midlands, after it came down to tangle in the trees. But if there is a hillside that overlooks the city, you can take me there."

He smiled, and vowed that he would someday have her aloft in one of those hot-air contrivances. Then the coach door opened and he descended, and turned to hand her out. But she paused in the carriage, staring up at his house to ask, a touch of awe in her tone, "What is this place?"

"Winters House," he said.

Reaching out, he fit his hands around her waist and lifted her down. She was far too busy gawking to pay any heed, so he allowed his hold to linger. She had a trim waist. A nice fit, indeed, for the span of his hands.

And then a voice behind him interrupted his thoughts before they could get properly started. "Well, I never!"

St. Albans turned to find his neighbor—Lady Monmouth—staring at him from her front steps. The door to her town house stood open behind her. The lanterns beside her doorway and his own illuminated her—and himself—quite clearly. As he watched, her ladyship's coach came around the corner and drew to a halt next to his own.

It had not occurred to him before, but now it did, that he was about to scandalize London. Gentlemen did not bring their mistresses home with them. No, they kept their *interesting connections* in separate houses in less fashionable neighborhoods, as if the loose morals of those women were somehow infectious.

But he did not want to install his Gypsy in a house elsewhere. After taking so much trouble to catch her, he wanted her close to him. So he had brought her to Grosvenor Square and Winters House, and if his neighbors did not care for such company, they could retire to their county estates a few weeks before the usual summer exodus.

Now, as he stared back at Lady Monmouth, who glared at him, and then glanced at his Gypsy as if she were a contagion, the devil inspired him.

Tipping his hat, he gave Lady Monmouth a slight bow. "Good evening, my lady. May I have the pleasure of presenting you to my new mistress?"

Beside him, Glynis drew in a breath. Lady Monmouth's eyes widened, and she drew her velvet evening cloak tighter about her.

"Well, I . . . I never!" she muttered again. Then, she turned away from St. Albans, her stare fixed on her own coach. Well, that was one more acquaintance with a dull dowager that would no longer bother him, he decided.

Amused, he turned back to find his Gypsy watching him, her stare reproachful. He lifted an eyebrow, and she shook her head.

"You are like some . . . some little boy who has to pull every petticoat you see, just to see the ladies jump."

"I beg your pardon. I thought you were here to pose as a mistress, and what better time to start than the present? Lady Monmouth will have the gossip spread before midnight. Now, would you care to dine?"

Glynis glanced up at him, and then at his even more

imposing house. All carved stone and glittering windows that would cost a fortune in window tax. Lanterns burned beside a double door large enough for 'Lisi and their cart to fit through with room to spare on each side. A black iron fence surrounded a tidy front garden where roses twined and leafed. It looked—well, it looked all too intimidating and grand.

However, his next words wiped away her hesitation about entering.

"And perhaps you would care to wash off the dust of traveling with a bath?"

SIX

"A bath?" she asked, the word conjuring images of a comfort she had almost forgotten existed.

A bath. A heated bath. In the summer, she bathed in whatever river lay nearest to their camp. In the winter, she sponged herself clean with water at least heated by the fire. But she had had a real bath once before.

As a child of four, on that awful night after Bado had saved them, when she had been caked with his blood and some of her own, her mother had taken them to an inn. Glynis shivered even now at those ancient, faded memories. But she could still remember the warmth of the water, and the smell of lavender soap, and how afterwards her mother had held her wrapped in something soft and she had felt safe then.

It was the last time she could remember feeling safe. For after that, they had always been traveling. Always looking back in case someone followed.

And now she followed the Earl, trailing after him and his promise of a bath. He led her into a hall so vast that she had to tip her head back to see the ceiling, which was painted with an intricate design, and at its center a knight rode a black horse. She stared around her. Everything seemed so impossibly elegant. White walls, rich tapestries, polished floors of black and white, a curved staircase with a red carpet that wound up its steps. It smelled sweet from beeswax and lemon oil and the fragrance of the spring flowers that spilled from the Chinese vase on a round table in the hall's center.

She pulled her cloak tighter, for her dress felt suddenly thin and drab, and she was aware of her ragged boots and the dirt under her fingernails.

"Where is the bath?" she asked, clutching her bundle. Her voice echoed in the hall, almost making her wish that she had spoken in a whisper. Ah, but she did not feel welcome here.

St. Albans turned from his two servants, tall men, though not as tall as he, she noted. They dressed in dark clothes, and they did not smile. The Earl had given them his hat and gloves. Now he waved them away, and then snapped his fingers.

A small, thin man strolled into the hall, his reddish hair brushed into gleaming curls. He dressed almost as well as the Earl, in a pale blue brocade waistcoat and a dark blue coat, white breeches, white stockings, and black shoes. He seemed to come from nowhere. Did these servants stand out of sight, waiting to be summoned?

"This is Gascoyne," St. Albans said, indicating the small man, who gave a deep bow to her as if she were a lady. "Gascoyne, this is Miss Glynis Chatwin. You will see to her comforts. She will have a bath, then we dine at ten."

"But of course, milord," Gascoyne said, his words lifted by a foreign-sounding accent. He bowed to her again, indicating the stairs with one hand. "If you will but follow me."

She almost wanted to stay with the Earl. Him, at least, she knew. But he was watching her, an amused smile turning his eyes a glittering green, and so she shot him a cool look that she hoped seemed sophisticated, and then started up the stairs.

Gascoyne led her up two flights to a room that opened into another room with a canopied bed large enough for a horse to sleep upon. She could not help but walk around, staring at everything, clutching her small bundle, which felt even smaller now.

The room smelled of flowers, and even though summer had not yet come, masses of red roses stood in vases. Decorated in gold and greens that accented the warm wood floors and paneling, the room looked as if someone had brought the woods inside. Delicate furniture, carved and curved, made up intimate corners for conversation beside a white marble fireplace, and near the long windows and the two tall bookcases.

Casually, she made her way to the windows and parted the drapes. But the windows looked out on the back gardens, not the square. Ah, well, she would find another way to let Christo know where she slept.

The man, Gascoyne, went around the room, lighting more candles, and she could only think how very expensive that must be. Then he turned to her. "Would mademoiselle care for tea?"

She could only nod. *He must be French,* she thought, feeling even more that she did not belong here in a place where even the servants were more refined than she.

Gascoyne gave her a bow, then went into the other room and opened the doors to an enormous wardrobe. "You will find all you need here. Milord ordered a little of everything to be bought today. And you have but to ring and a maid will come to help you dress."

A bath. A maid to dress. Tea brought to her.

She had to sit down on one of the chairs.

Ah, but it was worse than ever she had imagined. She

had not only to fight the earl and his charm. Now she had to fight the lure of all this as well.

Pushing back from the dinner table, St. Albans decided it had been a mistake not to order the meal in a more intimate setting. But he had wanted to impress her.

He had forgotten, however, that he had banished the ancestral portraits to the formal dining room, for when he entertained, it was always at his clubs, or at one of the more exclusive establishments in Covent Garden that catered to a gentleman's taste.

Well, she had been impressed, but in quite the wrong fashion.

She had come downstairs, clean, smelling of lilac soap, her skin rosy from her bath, but wearing that plain blue gown of hers. He had frowned at that. Well, no matter. The dressmaker would visit tomorrow, and while she was stripped and measured, he would have these rags burned. He would at least have her looking a proper mistress in something more provocative.

But then she had stepped into the dining room, her eyes had widened, and the questions started.

"Are all these your relatives? Ah, but I've never seen so many paintings. Who is that? Your mother? She looks very like you—very pretty. Or should I say that you look like her? Why do you not have any of your family with you?"

Such blunt interrogation left him rather unsettled. No one quizzed the Earl of St. Albans. And he certainly did not want to discuss his family. So he directed her to her chair, gave a vague answer, and began to talk instead of the delicacies he had arranged for her pleasure.

She had allowed herself to be seated, but then frowned at the table settings. "Why do you use so many forks and spoons? No wonder you need so many servants if they must clean all this. What is this small one for? Fish? Oh, thank you," she said, directing the last comment to the footman who had just ladled soup into her bowl.

Startled, the fellow had nearly dropped both the ladle and the Chinese porcelain tureen.

St. Albans leaned forward. "My dear, in polite company one does not notice the footmen who wait at table."

"Bah—that does not sound polite!" Twisting in her chair, she glanced up at the footman. "You—what is your name?"

The fellow turned a pale face to the Earl, and then shot a panicked glance at the butler.

St. Albans nodded at his butler, who in turn gave a nod to the footman, and a glance that clearly cautioned the man not to get too familiar with his betters, even with this invitation.

"James, miss," the footman said, his voice reedy and nervous.

She smiled up at him, and St. Albans thought crossly that she certainly seemed free enough with smiles for his staff.

"Well, James, tell me—and be honest—is it not always nicer to have a kind thank-you for your work?"

James swallowed hard, glanced at the earl and the butler once again, then straightened. "Yes, miss. It is nice."

Turning back, his Gypsy gave St. Albans a nod, as if she had proven herself in the right of things.

St. Albans gave up at that point. If his Gypsy wanted to flout social convention, he would allow it. In fact, she was rather like a spring wind through this musty house— a somewhat strong spring wind, but still refreshing. And if the staff took offense at her informality, well, then Gascoyne would be kept busy hiring new servants.

The questions continued with each course, for she asked him about any dish she could not recognize.

Her appetite impressed him, and he thought that he

had not been wrong about her. Life burned hot in her, and it was going to be a pleasure to warm his hands by such a fire.

As the last course was removed, St. Albans indicated that his Gypsy's wineglass should be refilled, and then he gave his butler, Palmer, a nod that the servants should leave the cheese and fruit on the table and retire.

Turning back to his Gypsy, he found her toying with her wineglass, one hand resting on her stomach and her stare fixed on the portraits again.

"Would you care for anything else?" he asked.

She shook her head, and then frowned. "You still have not said why none of your relatives live with you. Is it that you do not like them, or do they not like you?"

He offered her a blank stare, the empty one he reserved for such cheeky impertinence. She stared back at him, her expression expectant, either made immune by wine or left too confident by his easy treatment of her. Well, if she would not leave the subject gracefully, he would give her an answer that would close the topic.

"If you must know, my aunts—two were my late mother's sisters, and one from my father's side—generally prefer the countryside. Since they bestow on me the most ghastly presents—anything with too much gilt, or my crest upon it—I presume they do not hold me in utter disdain.

"As to my uncles, I have five. Four belong to my mother's family, and one is my father's younger brother. And they considered their job done with after having given me a succession of tutors, and then finishing my education with a full introduction to vice.

"Now, shall I continue with a list of my assorted cousins, second cousins and distant connections, or would you rather I read to you the full lineage from the most recent edition of *Debrett's Peerage and Baronetage?*"

She wrinkled her nose. "You are mocking my question. And I thought you wanted to charm me."

"That was before you became a disrespectful baggage."

Her eyes glittered. "*Became* disrespectful? As if I ever respected you to start with, my lord Earl."

Tilting her head, she lifted her wineglass to her lips, but kept her dark eyes on him. He could see the speculation in those enticing eyes.

"Now what? Are you thinking there must be some dark secret in my past?" He kept his tone flippant. In fact, he doubted if anyone's life was as open as his. And why not? His family never dared criticize him, for he was, after all, the Earl of St. Albans, and as for the rest of the world, he had no interest in either its good opinion or even its right to judge him.

His Gypsy stared at him, her eyes wide and dark, as if taking his full measure, and that set his temper to simmering.

"What, do you think that I must live a sad, empty life not to have my family close about me? That I have wealth and little else? Do allow me to assure you that I lack for nothing."

"You lack for parents."

He stilled instantly. Oh, but she did have a sharp tongue to so expertly lay bare a scar so old that he had gone for years without remarking it. He forced himself to relax. He had long ago learned not to look into that darkness. And she was not about to bring any of it back to him.

That he would not allow.

Lifting one hand, he waved the matter away. "I am hardly a poor orphan. Now, shall we retire to a more comfortable room?"

He rose and held out his hand. She hesitated, still

measuring him, but then she put down her wineglass and rose to give him her hand.

He took her into the smaller drawing room that overlooked the street. A fire crackled in the grate and only a few candles burned. The intimate space offered only a low couch beside the fire and two small side tables.

Seating herself on the couch, she folded her hands in her lap. "Tell me about your parents. Did you know them at all?"

Exasperated, he stood before the fire, his hands folded behind his back and almost tempted to toss her onto the streets. Was this her method of preventing seduction? If so, it certainly was remarkably effective.

Staring down at her, he lifted an eyebrow and said nothing, but the look he had mastered for leaving the haughtiest dowager fluttering seemed to have no effect on her. It must be the wine, he decided. It had gone to her tongue.

He let out a sigh. "Very well, my curious Gypsy. If I satisfy you on this *last* question, do you vow that we can then allow this topic to rest?"

She nodded, then tucked her feet underneath her and snuggled into the pillows of the couch as if expecting a rare treat.

"Very well, then. But no interruptions with more questions, mind. And there is little enough to tell. My acquaintance with my mother lasted a day. And my father quite wisely quit this earth three days before my arrival. Nothing terribly dramatic, I assure you. He broke his neck on the hunt field, and my mother went into a decline. At least that was how my aunts put it. My uncles told me rather more graphically when I was six that she bled to death from the birthing."

"What! Do you mean they allowed you to think you caused her death?"

His mouth twisted. "I doubt that was their intent. At

the time, I had cut myself on my father's sword and they feared I might be a bleeder as well." He held up his left hand to show the white line of a scar that crossed his palm. "I am happy to say, I am not. As to my parents' death . . . well, accidents happen and people die. That is simply the way of the world. And the world and I long ago came to terms with each other."

Shocked, she stared at him. The wine had dulled her mind, but it did nothing to ease the tightness that gathered around her heart. The way of the world, he called it, as if things happened blindly. Well, it was not the way of her world. Yes, fate could be cruel. But it was not mindless. A pattern lay in the cloth of all events. Her mother had taught her that, and she clung to that belief fiercely.

But this one, ah, he saw only an indifferent world.

Scowling at him, she tried to think him cold for how he spoke, with that mocking distance in his voice. But she kept thinking instead that something else also lay behind this cold wall that he used to keep himself so removed from others.

She knew what it was to lose a parent. But she had vague memories of her father's arms about her, the smell of his cologne—spicy and warm—of his voice, rough and deep. And she had her mother's stories of him.

Ah, was this earl a man who stole hearts because he feared giving his own? And why did he so fear the healing warmth of love? Because it had been taken too often from him? Or never given, perhaps?

"Why are you not married?" she demanded suddenly.

For a moment, he simply stared at her. And then he surprised her by giving a laugh. A real laugh, one that reached his eyes, and transformed his face.

Oh, no, don't laugh, gaujo—you are dangerous enough when you smile, she thought, struggling to resist that wicked charm.

Sobering, he smiled down at her. "Have you, my Gypsy, never heard that it is impolite to badger a person with so many inopportune questions?"

She shrugged. "Well, you know about me already—that I am the daughter of a nobleman and a Gypsy. I could tell you that I dance like my mother, and that she has the gift of second sight—ah, but you see! You raise that eyebrow at me, and give me that look, which tells me that you think I am only making up another *swato*. So, what am I to talk about, if not you? Would you rather that I ask you when will you get me into Lord Nevin's house?"

"Patience, my dear. We must entice his interest in you, and not allow him to see your interest in him. But we will start tomorrow—when we are both better rested."

She almost told him that now he sounded like her mother, but there was wisdom in his advice. However, time favored him. Time to charm her. Time to weaken her with soft beds, and delicious food, and hot baths.

Well, she would not weaken. She would take what he offered, enjoy it, and leave him with his empty house and his empty heart.

Rising, she stood in front of him. "Until tomorrow, then."

He smiled at her and took her hand, and she braced herself for his kiss. He stood very close to her, his touch warm on her skin, his thumb brushing her palm in a way that set her blood singing.

But he only let go of her hand, and a sharp disappointment rose in her chest.

Go, you fool, go while you can, she told herself.

And then, before she could think better of it, she darted forward to press her lips to his cheek. Then she pulled away and hurried from the room, not daring to look back, scolding herself for her weakness. So what if he had been kind to her tonight—he did so only because he wanted something from her. But she would never forget that for this night he honestly had been kind. And for that she owed him more than a kiss.

St. Albans stood with a hand to his cheek, watching as his Gypsy slipped from the room and then let her steps quicken to a run. He watched until she was gone from sight, and then he stood there, his expression unchanged, his mood uncertain.

What had she meant by that kiss?

He would throttle her if she felt an ounce of pity for him. He needed no man's—or woman's—pity. He had everything he wanted. Or he would, once he had full possession of her.

But it crossed his mind to wonder if he wasn't playing a rather dangerous game here.

He began to smile. Would that not serve him well if he fell in love with her? What a splendid irony that would be. His smile faded, however, for the truth was he was far too much a realist to ever delude himself into believing in love.

Glynis found her way to her room quite easily. She had learned young always to remark her path—inside a house, or inside a woodland. Safety lay in knowledge.

But did it?

She had learned too much about this *gaujo* tonight, she thought, her head spinning with his wine, and her heart confused. He was no longer just a *gaujo*. Oh, yes, he was the Earl of St. Albans. But as she pulled off her dress and corset, and then slipped between sheets softer than any she had ever felt, she kept thinking about a boy with no parents, and such a very long title to wear and a very large house to live in alone.

Sleep came slowly, and troubled.

* * *

The couple ran from the church, laughing, hand clutching hand, him hatless and her with a red scarf that fell from her streaming dark hair. On the church steps, the vicar waved after them, and a farmer and his wife watched, the wife wiping her eyes, the farmer dour and shaking his head over such folly.

Glynis shifted in her sleep.

Running with the lovers, smiling for them, she followed as the woods rose up around them—around her— deep and silent and green. Laughing, they tumbled into the grass in a small glade, and she lay under the oak, staring up at blue sky until a face rose over her—a man with Christo's eyes.

She let out a sigh, a deep breath, as he leaned close. The world shifted softly, so that the man who lay with her now stared down at her with a different face, one she almost knew, his green eyes not yet cynical, his face still young and unmarked by life.

Smiling, she lifted her lips to his. As his mouth opened against hers, warmth curled inside her and kindled into something more.

And the voice echoed in her mind—her voice and yet not hers. "I have faith. I know you will do right and tell everyone about our love someday. Someday . . . some . . ."

A crack like a pistol shot woke her.

With a jerk, Glynis sat upright, clutching the bed-clothes, her breath caught in her chest, her face hot and her heart pounding.

The maid at the window blushed deeply. "Beg pardon, miss. I meant only to open the drapery to let the light wake you. His lordship said you wasn't to sleep late, for it's to be a full day. Would you care for tea or hot chocolate for breakfast?"

Glynis rubbed the sleep from her eyes, shot a suspicious glance at the iron curtain rings that had rattled on the curtain rod, and then muttered a request for tea.

Dropping a curtsy, the maid left, and Glynis lay back again, a hand across her eyes.

She felt as if she had been running all night, not sleeping. Closing her eyes, she struggled to catch the wisps of her dream. It seemed so important to remember it all.

The couple from the church, ah, yes, her parents. Had it not been they? Her forehead knotted.

She could understand why she should dream of her parents—particularly after last night's conversation with Lord St. Albans. But that kiss . . .

Brushing her fingertips across her lips, she wondered why she dreamed not of her father kissing her mother, but of St. Albans kissing her in the woods.

With a groan, she turned her face into the lavender-scented feather pillow.

Bad enough to have to resist his charm during the day, but did she have to fight her own dreams as well?

But she could not escape the feeling that lay in her bones and wrapped around her still from her dream that he had once loved a woman deeply. And the shadow of it lay over him still.

Ah, but he was a man who lived in too many shadows, so many that sunlight never would warm his heart, and she would do best to remember that.

With that in mind, she rose to dress for the day, and to see what plans this high and mighty lord had for her.

Everything changed—too much so, all too fast. And it was all she could do to remember that there was a pattern to it—a reason why she must endure.

The Earl brought a short, giddy blond woman to measure her for dresses, and a man who smelled of too much rose scent to cut her hair—which she refused.

His servants tried to steal her faded blue gown, so that she had to sneak down two nights in a row to take it back. The third time she caught Gascoyne with it, and so she showed him the pistol St. Albans had given her and promised to shoot the next person who touched her dress.

That she would not give up. It was a tenuous tie to her real self—her real life.

Ah, but this took more courage than she had thought it would, to step into this earl's world and have everything about her change into nothing she knew.

Except for the Earl of St. Albans.

A kind word, a sympathetic look, and she would have been in his arms. The thought of it tempted as nothing ever had in her life. Her throat ached with the need for comforting arms about her. And in the dark of her room at night, she curled up tight and lay there, her eyes open, telling herself this would not go on forever, and feeling so very alone.

If it had been only for herself, she would have fled. She would have run back to her Gypsy life and would have forgotten the fine clothes that lay light as gossamer on her skin. She would have left the soft bed, and the foods whose smells made her mouth water. She would have even left the hot baths behind.

She ached for something familiar. The hard ground. The owl's hoot, and the crow's sharp caw. The smell of the air after rain. She wanted something to hold onto, for she felt as if she was falling. And she wanted someone to hold her and to tell her that it would be all right.

Ah, but it would not. Not until this was done. Fate had put her feet upon a path and she must ask God to give her the strength to walk forward.

And all the while her *gaujo* smiled so charmingly, and acted as if he lived for nothing other than to please her.

When her new clothes arrived—clothes that fit her

almost too well, she thought, for they showed every curve of her body—he took her driving in the park. She craned for a glimpse of Lord Nevin's carriage, but St. Albans merely smiled and told her to be patient.

Bah—patience! If—when—this ever ended, she wanted never to hear the word again.

And the Earl took her out with him in the evening, to places that left Glynis's eyes wide at how little the women wore. She stayed very close to St. Albans on those nights, for she did not like the look in other men's eyes as they stared at her in her low-cut silk gown. She glared back at them until they grew uncomfortable and turned away. And she knew that when this was all over it would be a relief to live anyplace in England except this city that smelled of too many horses and people and chimneys. She longed even more for a simple house in a simple village.

Each night, she left her bedchamber windows open, and peered out into the darkness before retiring.

But Christo did not come.

Had he lost track of them? Had something happened to him? She fretted even more about that.

On her sixth night with St. Albans, she pleaded a headache after their drive—he had made good on his promise that day to take her about London, and had done so, spending the whole day on her, as attentive as any girl could wish for. He had smiled at her, and had even made her laugh with his comments, and she knew that she could not dine with him alone that night.

She was starting to like his company too much. She was starting, in fact, to crave his presence. To depend on him. And that was not a safe thing at all, she knew.

So she told him she was tired, and she gave him a smile; then she fled, her heart in her throat, half wishing he would follow her up to her room.

He did not.

Rake! What sort of rake was he that he left a woman alone in her chamber night after night, her bed empty of anything but those dreams that plagued her.

Ah, but it was better this way, she told herself fiercely as she brushed out her hair. She had learned to allow the maid to help her dress, but she undressed herself. It was the one pattern left from her old life. She clung to it as dearly as she held onto her worn blue gown.

Wrapping herself in one of the high-waisted brocade dressing gowns that the Earl had provided, she opened the window and leaned her elbows on the sill. The faint sweetness of jasmine lay in the air, offering a promise of summer heat soon to come. Spring was slipping by so fast.

Going back to her bed, she curled up, her candle still lit.

She did not want to sleep, and while she had raided his lordship's library for a selection of novels, none of them appealed tonight. She wanted company. She wanted to talk to someone—to St. Albans, in fact. She wanted to tell him more of her life, and she wanted to ask him about his.

She wanted to trust him.

"Oh, don't be a fool," she muttered to herself.

Then she heard the scrabbling noise outside her window.

Getting up, she padded across the floor and peered outside. Her heart lightened as she glimpsed familiar broad shoulders, and then her pulse raced as she saw how perilously he clung to the ivy that climbed the wall beside her window.

"Are you going to help me, or are you, too fine a lady for that now?" Christo growled.

"Hush. You'll wake someone," she said, already taking hold of his arm.

The vine trembled as if the trellis would collapse, but

Christo grabbed for her window and caught the ledge. Grasping his belt, she pulled him in, so that they tumbled into the room with him on top of her.

Immediately, she swatted at him. "What took you so long?" Then she wrapped her arms around him. "Ah, I've missed you so."

"Dromboy tume, Romanle," he said, offering the Romany greeting with a smile in his voice and his arms tight about her.

And then a deep, lazy voice from the doorway cut across her joy, and she could not mistake the icy anger that lay underneath. "My dear, if you wish to have visitors, I must insist that you invite them in through the front door."

SEVEN

St. Albans lowered his pistol. After Gascoyne had alerted him that an intruder had entered the gardens, he'd had a suspicion he would find this Gypsy fellow here, and caution seemed in order. It was a touch tempting, however, to shoot the fellow and toss his lifeless body out the window. But, to judge by his Gypsy's welcome for the fellow, he could not do that without alienating her affections. So he would have to endure.

His Gypsy rose to her feet, as did her companion, moving with easy athleticism. "I didn't think I would be welcome," the fellow said, his tone insolent and his expression even more so.

St. Albans raised an eyebrow, then turned to Glynis. "You are hardly a prisoner. And while I have been aware that your . . ."

He hesitated for an accurate description, and as he did, his Gypsy's chin rose. "My Lord St. Albans, I think it is time you formally met my brother, Christopher Chatwin Dawes—the rightful Lord Nevin."

The rest of St. Albans's prepared speech went out of his head. Every muscle stilled. And then an unaccountable relief mixed with his astonishment.

The rightful Lord Nevin? What in blazes would she be inventing next—castles in the sky? And yet . . . had she not said that she was after an inheritance from Nevin? Hers and her brother's, it seemed.

At the moment, her brother was hissing something at her in his Gypsy tongue, and she was answering back, her eyes dark and flashing.

A brother, eh? The tension eased from St. Albans's shoulders. The fellow would no doubt prove a nuisance—family always was—but he had disliked excessively the thought that his Gypsy might be sneaking a lover into Winters House.

"I do hate to interrupt this family squabble," he said. "But I suggest brandy, a fire, and then explanations."

Without waiting for any agreement, he moved to the bellpull. His Gypsy's brother began to mutter something else to her, and after ringing for Gascoyne, St. Albans gave the fellow a cold stare. "And you may either keep quiet, or speak for all to hear. I have had enough of your poor manners."

The man's jaw tensed and he glared at St. Albans, but the Earl took no notice. He still held his pistol, after all, so let the fellow be surly. However, he was done with them sharing secrets in their Gypsy language.

Gascoyne arrived, prompt as ever.

Giving orders for a fire to be laid and brandy to be brought, St. Albans put his pistol on the mantel in the salon and waited for more candles to be lit.

When they were comfortable enough—the fire blazing, glasses and decanter on a satinwood drum table, his Gypsy curled up on the couch with her brother next to her—St. Albans leaned against the mantel, within reach of his pistol. His Gypsy's brother, after all, had come rather close to skewering him, and the fellow's black eyes still glittered darkly.

"Now, you may explain this claim of yours," St. Albans said.

Silence greeted him as brother and sister exchanged a glance, the brother's stare glowering and suspicious, the sister's questioning.

Now that he was looking at them, St. Albans saw the strong resemblances between these two. Not just in dark coloring, but in the arch of eyebrows, the strong nose and high cheekbones, the slanting shape of their eyes. Glynis was far more fetching—her features more refined, her ears small, her chin more rounded—but this Gypsy fellow would clean up well enough if his hair was trimmed, the dark stubble on his cheeks shaved off, and his clothes cut to fit.

As the silence stretched, so that only the hiss of coal burning filled the room, St. Albans gave a small sigh. It would have to be up to him, it seemed. "There is no point in keeping anything from me. I have my own ways of finding the truth. For example, I am well aware that your brother here has been skulking about for the past few days."

"I was not skulking," Christo said, teeth gritted. "I was keeping a watch."

"Well, if you were doing the same with Lord Nevin, you have no doubt set his staff on alert as well."

The Gypsy fellow gave a derisive snort. "Those fools. They know nothing."

"Arrogant of you to think so. However, I will grant that Lord Nevin is—"

"He is not Lord Nevin, my brother—"

St. Albans held up a hand. "Yes, I know, your brother claims that title—the imperative word here being *claims*. However, to prevent argument, we shall keep to given names and leave titles out of it. And while Francis Dawes—whom you claim for an uncle—is no doubt full of his own conceit, he does not lack intelligence. If you were lucky, his staff took you for no more than just another garden-variety thief."

The impudent fellow smiled and leaned back. "My sister is the one with the light fingers in the family."

St. Albans's irritation with this fellow deepened. He

lounged here, brandy glass in hand, as if he honestly were a lord. Instead, he was likely an imposter, a liar, and very much as bad as his host.

So what did that make his sister?

Glancing at his Gypsy, St. Albans found her frowning at a pillow, tugging on its gold trim, and uncharacteristically quiet. If he did not know better, he might have thought her pensive stare held a touch of shame at this mention of her past. That seemed unlike her. But he found he also did not like her to be made uncomfortable.

St. Albans turned back to the brother. "I am well aware of your sister's . . . borrowing abilities." He smiled, recalling how they had met—and how she had looked half undressed. And then he fought to put his attention back on the moment. "That is not under discussion. What I wish to hear from you is as much of the truth as can fall from your lips. Just who was your father, and why should you think you are legitimate heirs of the Dawes family?"

The fellow's black eyes glittered again, hostile and bright. With his disheveled hair and jaw shadowed by beard, he looked a hang-gallows. "Why should we tell you anything?"

St. Albans smiled. "Because you are both in my power, and I can deal you harm, or good, as my whim takes me. It is quite up to you which direction I am swayed."

"Let me tell him, Christo. It is time. And he has no reason to betray us."

Pressing his lips thin, St. Albans kept back the words that slipped into his mind. In truth, he had every reason to prefer that his Gypsy remain a Gypsy. If she became the recognized, legitimate sister of the Baron of Nevin, that gave her a measure of protection from him that he would just as soon she not have.

However, he had never allowed a lady's birth or status

to interfere with her ruination—not if the lady willingly participated. But it was an uncomfortable thought that she might not be the wild Gypsy that he wanted her to be.

"Well?" he asked. Pulling out his snuffbox, he helped himself to a delicate pinch. It was a habit he had taken up over a decade ago, when he first came to town and shortly after the one disastrous entanglement of his life. Its use really was more as a prop, something to do with his hands, so that he never fidgeted, a habit he had deplored in himself when he was as young as these two.

His Gypsy shot her brother a glance. The fellow looked as if he wanted to say something—no doubt in Gypsy. St. Albans kept his stare fixed on the fellow. He really would shoot him if he said a word that was not in English. The fellow's jaw worked, then his mouth pulled down and he waved his hand, as if resigned.

Glynis turned back to St. Albans, an expression of relief upon her face, as if this were a secret that had become too heavy to carry.

"My father was Edward Dawes—the late Lord Nevin's eldest son. He married my mother—honestly married her—at a small church in the village of Nevin, near to the Welsh border."

"And how do you know this—your mother told you?" St. Albans asked, trying to keep the skepticism from his voice.

Christo stiffened. "Are you saying our mother is a—"

"Christo, he is only asking! And, yes, she did tell us. But she also showed us her wedding ring."

"Ah, iron—or in this case, gold—clad proof."

"If we had proof, *gaujo,* we would not be here. This is useless, *Phen!* This one, he would find lies more believable."

St. Albans regarded the young hothead with dispassion. "Please, do feel free to leave at anytime."

For a moment, the Gypsy fellow glowered, his body tensed as if he would fling himself from the room. But then he glanced at his sister's worried expression and leaned back against the couch again, his brandy clenched in his hand.

"I'll stay, *gaujo*."

St. Albans turned to his Gypsy girl. "For argument's sake, we shall assume that *a* marriage took place. It is not unknown, however, for such unions to be—shall we say, right-handed affairs? And very far from legal. Did your father ever do anything to recognize you, or take you to his family? And why did your mother not come forward years ago?"

Glynis's face darkened. "You met Bado. You saw the scar on his face. And you have met my mother."

St. Albans frowned. "Yes, but what—"

"Francis Dawes gave him that face, the night Bado saved my life, and Christo's and my mother's, from Dawes's men. And a club swung by one of his men struck my mother and stole her sight. To him, a pair of *poshrats*—half Gypsies such as we—are a cancer to be cut out." She leaned forward, her expression intent, her eyes black pools. "Now tell me that my mother was wrong to hide us from a man who by law would have been given his brother's children to raise. I was four, Christo one. Tell me we could do anything but hide until we both came of age and were strong enough to challenge him."

St. Albans swirled his brandy. Well, that part of her story he could believe. Particularly if, after Edward Dawes had died, the mother had gone looking for what she could get from the estate. It would be like Francis Dawes to think himself doing right by the world to rid it of a few such inconvenient, dirty Gypsies.

However, a few details remained unexplained, such as why would any Dawes marry so far beneath him? St.

Albans had had no acquaintance with Edward Dawes, but he found it difficult to believe that a man of his class would look for a wife in the woods.

Of course, here was his own Gypsy, looking desirable as sin. If her mother had been anything like this, he could see the attraction that Edward Dawes would have felt. But a legal marriage? Why, the man would have had to have been ready to give up the world—his own world.

That seemed quite unlikely.

However, what mattered was that his Gypsy believed this tale.

She stared up at him, her wide mouth fixed with determination, her dressing gown parting slightly to show that tempting valley between her breasts where he so ached to rest his head.

And there seemed but a single method to rid her mind of this obsession.

He was going to have to get that blasted box into her hands so that she could see it contained no legal marriage lines. He was going to have to ruin her dreams, and then he could show her how to take what pleasure she could from this life.

Of course, her being an illegitimate Dawes offered a certain appeal—no wonder she had the look of quality upon her face and her voice. And he would convince her that she could still have revenge upon Nevin through lording it over London as the Earl of St. Albans's mistress. Yes, that would be amusing for them both.

Only something about the scheme troubled him still, and he was in no mood to pry into his own feelings on the matter. He wanted her. He had sworn he would have her. By any means.

And that settled that.

Tossing back his brandy, he set his glass down, then strode to the bellpull to summon Gascoyne. He could feel his Gypsy's eyes on him as he moved, but he avoided meeting her gaze.

Gascoyne arrived, and St. Albans turned to him, annoyed and not even certain why he should be so, other than that this seduction seemed to be becoming a damnable tangle.

"Miss Chatwin's brother will be staying with us, Gascoyne. See that the green room is readied for him." St. Albans turned to his pair of Gypsies. "I think we have all had enough stimulation tonight. Tomorrow I shall give you a far better plan than skulking about Nevin's house."

"I was not skulking," the Gypsy said again, and at the same time his sister said, "A plan? What is it?"

St. Albans ignored the brother and gave a tight smile to the sister, whose eager questions had managed to tease some of his ill humor from him. She would no doubt go to the grave questioning Death himself.

"Well, my dear," he said. "For a start, I am going to take you to the Cyprian's Ball next week."

"Prostitutes! He wants you to become one of them, and he thinks by taking you to this—"

"Bah! I know what he thinks. But if he says he has a plan, then do not underestimate him, Christo. He is a lord. An earl. He can help us if he so chooses."

Christopher glowered at his sister. They stood in the salon adjacent to her bedchamber, with coffee and tea and delicate china laid out on a mahogany drop-leaf table beside the window. Sunlight streamed in from between the parted, green velvet drapery, and a light breeze carried the promise of summer's coming.

Hunching a shoulder, Christopher scowled, his dark eyes black as night. "It is not his help that I doubt. It is the price he will want for it. That one thinks the world is his to order. Don't trust him, *Phen.*"

Glynis looked down into her teacup. It was a measure of Christo's agitation that he spoke in Romany to her now, and used the Rom for *sister*. He worried for her. Rightly so. But the Earl had said that he knew how to ensure that Francis Dawes would be at the Cyprian's Ball. For that, Glynis would risk anything.

Even herself.

She had to make certain that Christo found his place in this world. For without it, she saw as clearly as her mother saw in the cards that he could become a bitter, hard man.

Looking up at him, she smiled. "A fine one you are to urge caution. You were the one who risked hanging when you stole that fine stallion from Nevin, after *Dej* told us the truth this spring about how our father died."

Christo gave a grim smile. "I cannot steal what should have been mine by rights. But what will this *gaujo* steal from you?" He came to her side and put his wide hand on her shoulder. She felt his strength ease into her. His hard grip and calluses reminded her of the years they had worked side by side simply to survive.

"Be careful, *Phen*. It is not how this *gaujo* looks at you that tightens my heart. It is how you watch him."

She forced a smile and covered his hand with hers. "Of course I watch him. I watch this one very carefully."

A soft tap on the door made them both turn; Gascoyne entered, his bow polite. Glynis had noted that since that last time she had taken back her blue gown, he had treated her with almost the same deference he gave the Earl.

I could like being a lady, she thought. Only she was not much of one, really. Ladies did not grow up running wild in the woods, learning to shoot and skin rabbits. They did not know how to light campfires with flint, and did not dance under the full moon. They did not steal from others with guilty hearts, and they did not pose as a scoundrel's mistress.

Well, she had done what she must. She had helped keep her family from going hungry, or getting sick. Now her skills—and her ability to handle the Earl of St. Albans—could make the difference in helping Christo regain his title. Then she could leave this city and find her quiet village and the life she wanted.

So, when Gascoyne said that the earl waited for her downstairs, she rose, said she would dress at once, and join him in fifteen minutes.

It took twenty-five, because her maid argued with her about what she was to wear. Glynis saw no reason not to don her blue gown. It was the best she owned, and she only wore the gowns the Earl had had made for her when she was to be seen with him in public.

However, when the maid began to look fearful, insisting that the earl had requested riding attire, Glynis submitted. The dress clung to every curve, and she secretly loved the fabric, a wool so soft and light that it seemed alive. Black braid trimmed the gray habit, and it had a matching shako that delighted her. She knew she looked well in it, but she found it hard to think of herself as anything but a barefoot, ragged Gypsy.

When she came downstairs, she found the Earl waiting for her, standing quite still and staring at the clock in the hall, his hands folded behind his back and tapping his riding crop on the back of his boots. His black coat and riding breeches contrasted sharply with his golden hair and his white shirt and buff waistcoat.

She bit her lower lip, then came down the stairs. "I hate being late. I am sorry."

He turned and smiled, his expression amused, the corner of his mouth quirking. "I thought you enjoyed making me wait." He took her hand. "For everything."

Keeping his stare locked with hers, he raised her hand, then turned it over and pressed his lips to her palm.

Heat shot from the touch of his mouth, up her arm and then pooled deep inside her. She struggled to hide her reaction, but she saw satisfaction glimmer in his eyes.

She frowned at him and pulled her hand away. "I only know one way to ride—astride, without a saddle." "Then you have something new to learn."

He bowed, indicating for her to step outside. She did so, and then stopped on the top step to stare into the square.

A groom led St. Albans's black horse up and down the pavement. Next to the large animal walked a smaller one, dainty with huge dark eyes, delicate hooves, and an equally black coat.

Glynis glanced at the Earl. "Do you not own a single horse that is not black?"

His mouth quirked. "No. I do not. It is one of my conceits. Now come meet Martif. She is a half-breed, like you, so you already have that in common. And she is almost pony-sized, although you will have to ride side saddle, unless you would rather shock London by doing without all that leather."

Glynis wrinkled her nose and thought about it. In truth, she was not a very good rider. Christo was far better. She did not get enough practice, and she preferred their pony 'Lisi, with her broad back and comfortable paces, to the bad-mannered horses that Christo bought to retrain.

However, she did not want to show any weakness in front of the Earl, so she gave a shrug. "It does not matter. But why are we riding? Why not drive? And why so early in the day?"

"Always questions. Well, this time, my sweet torment, you must wait until you're mounted to have your answers."

He led her down the steps and then took her by the waist before she could do more than open her mouth to protest. His hands tightened and her breath seemed to lodge near her heart. Then he lifted her into the saddle as if she weighed nothing.

The black mare stood quite still, as patient as if a baby had been placed upon her. Gratitude warmed Glynis, for both the mare's steadiness and St. Albans's hold. With both of her legs dangling on one side of the horse, she felt as if she could tip off the other side if she so much as leaned an inch in that direction.

St. Albans gave her instructions. Sit straight, not twisted. Keep her balance in her seat. He put her foot into the single stirrup, and made certain her right leg hooked over the single pommel horn. She was too busy trying to sort everything out to do more than absently notice how his hands seemed to touch her everywhere.

When he had her seated to please himself, he strode to his own black gelding and swung lightly into the saddle, looking very pleased with himself and the world.

She envied how easily he did that, and wondered if he would teach her that trick of swinging up without the stirrups. Even getting on stout 'Lisi usually involved a lot of struggling, wiggling, and breath-stealing effort on her part.

"Now, shall we ride to the park and talk about your attire for the Cyprian's Ball? It's fancy dress, and should be something to attract Nevin's—beg pardon, I mean Francis Dawes's—attention."

Her horse placidly fell into step next to St. Albans's mount, and for a moment Glynis had to concentrate on the odd sensation of being seated sideways. But her black mare moved like spring water—fresh and smooth. She began to relax.

Tilting her head, she studied St. Albans. "You went to

all this trouble to take me from the house to talk about this ball? Why—because of Christo?"

The lines around his eyes tightened. "He is—"

"Hot-tempered? Yes, I know. Difficult also. And perhaps also, for you, inconvenient?"

His smile widened. "Very. But I do not want to spend this lovely day talking about him. Here are the gates. Do you feel able to do more than sit a walk?"

That lovely chin lifted, as St. Albans had known it would. His Gypsy could pass up many things, but not a challenge. She was like him in that fashion.

"Of course," she said, although he noted with a smile that she wrapped a few surreptitious fingers into the mare's black mane.

He spurred Cinder to a slow canter, knowing the mare would follow. It was a fast pace, but a smoother gait than the bouncy trot. For a moment, Glynis's face paled, but as her mare moved steady and sure, she began to smile. And then she gave a laugh of pure delight.

Lust, pure and uncomplicated, shot through St. Albans. And a curious tightness gathered in his chest as well. He frowned at himself and looked away, uneasy, but his stare found its own way back to his Gypsy.

Why am I taking so long with this? Why do I give her such patience?

Now he sounded like his Gypsy—all questions. And that irritated him. He had set the pace, he reminded himself. Did not the story of Tantalus show that it was those things just out of reach that tempted the most? He wanted her tempted—tempted and teased and tormented.

Slowing his mount to a walk, he gave her a smile.

She leaned down to pat her mare, and then beamed at him. "Ah, but Christo would love this one. Only we are not to talk of him, are we? Well, then tell me what you are thinking now—you have that pleased-with-your-own-cleverness smile."

"I was thinking of the story Tantalus. Do you know it? He lived in ancient times, and when he displeased the gods, they condemned him to live forever in water to his chin, so that when he bent to drink, the water fell away. And when he rose up to eat, the wind pushed the sweet, luscious grapes overhead just out of his reach."

She brushed the black mare's mane. "But if he was to live forever anyway, he did not really need food or water, did he?"

St. Albans's mouth twitched. "That is not the point of the story."

She lifted one shoulder. "It sounds to me as if it is. He did not need food and water—he just wanted it. I wonder sometimes, which is worse, to want something desperately—or to get it? I worry for Christo sometimes that way. He wants his place in this world so desperately. Only perhaps he wants it too much. What will he do with it when he has it?"

Frustration simmered in St. Albans's chest. He had known this brother's appearance would be a bother. And now he could not even flirt properly with his Gypsy.

Reaching out, he covered her hands with one of his, pulling her mount and his to a halt. "I would rather know what it is that would make *you* desperate with desire?"

She smiled up at him, and his senses danced.

"My desires? Ah, they are so simple, you would laugh."

"Would I? Try me."

She glanced at him, her dark eyes uncertain, and she slipped her hands out from his and turned her attention to brushing her mare's arched neck. "All I have ever wanted is a house. A cottage really, with a garden. And a cow. And maybe a cat, too. And it should have a sitting room with a fireplace that looks into the garden, and it should be in a small village—a place where I belong, where people know me and accept me."

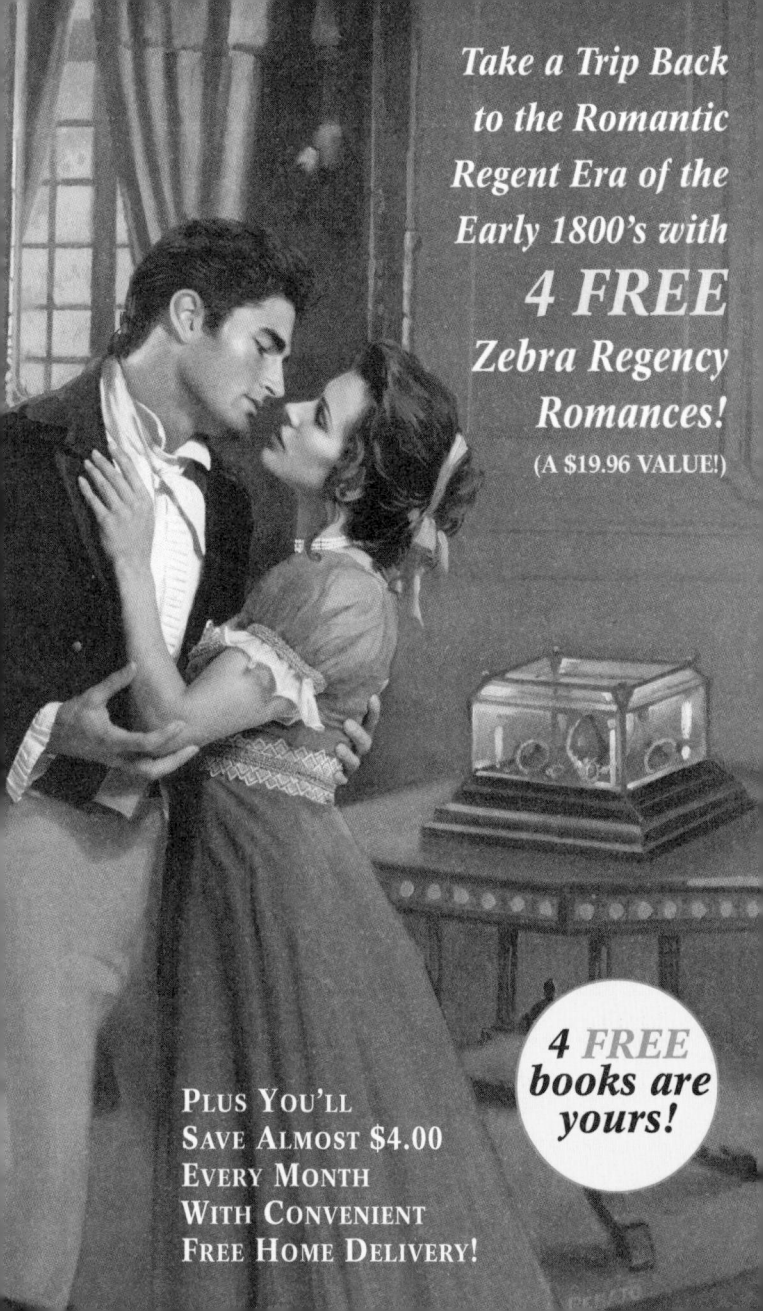

Take a Trip Back to the Romantic Regent Era of the Early 1800's with

4 FREE
Zebra Regency Romances!

(A $19.96 VALUE!)

4 *FREE* books are yours!

We'd Like to Invite You to Subscribe to Zebra's Regency Romance Book Club and Give You a Gift of 4 Free Books as Your Introduction! (Worth $19.96!)

If you're a Regency lover, imagine the joy of getting 4 FREE Zebra Regency Romances and then the chance to have these lovely stories delivered to your home each month at the lowest price available! Well, that's our offer to you and here's how you benefit by becoming a Regency Romance subscriber:

- **4 FREE** Introductory Regency Romances are delivered to your doorstep

- 4 BRAND NEW Regencies are then delivered each month (usually before they're available in bookstores)

- Subscribers save almost $4.00 every month

- You also receive a **FREE** monthly newsletter, which features author profiles, discounts, subscriber benefits, book previews and more

- No risks or obligations...in other words, you can cancel whenever you wish with no questions asked

Join the thousands of readers who enjoy the savings and convenience offered to Regency Romance subscribers. After your initial introductory shipment, you receive 4 brand-new Zebra Regency Romances each month to examine for 10 days. Then, if you decide to keep the books, you'll pay the preferred subscriber's price.

It's a no-lose proposition, so return the FREE BOOK CERTIFICATE today!

She glanced up at him, her chin lowered, and her dark eyes huge. "There. I told you it would seem as nothing to you, but to me, it is all I have dreamed of since I was a girl."

He stared at her, and then said, his voice rough to his own ears, "I could give you that."

She looked at him, a hard edge of mocking laughter in her eyes. "Oh, yes, you would like to give me a cottage, wouldn't you? And would you also buy me a warm welcome from those who lived there, so they would not scorn your mistress?"

He glared at her. That was not what he had meant. Or had he? His anger began to simmer. "There are ways to do these things without occasioning talk. Besides, what does it matter to you what others think?"

"So long as I get what I want, you mean? Well, you may not care about anyone else's feelings, *gaujo*. I am not made that way. I do care. I am an outsider by birth, but I am going to find a way to belong someplace, *gaujo!* And I will find that without the strings on one of your gifts."

Spurring her mount forward, she pulled away, angry with him for mocking her dreams. He had no intention, she knew, of giving. No, she saw how he tempted her now with his offer—and how later he would want something from her in return. It was a bargain he offered her, not a gift. And it shamed her that part of her anger came from a desire to take it.

He rode after her, but she would not look back and would not slow to talk to him. She did not rein up until they were before Winters House again, and then she slipped off her mount without waiting for assistance.

A footman hurried from the house to take the horses, and St. Albans tossed Cinder's reins to the fellow and strode after his Gypsy, his temper in tatters.

How dare she speak to him in such a fashion! How

dare she criticize him! And how dare she turn away from him, dismissing him as if he were some . . . some lackey.

In the hall, he took hold of her elbow and swung her around, then he took her chin in his gloved hand. She tried to wrench away, but he tightened his grip, forcing her face upward until she had to look at him. Her eyes blazed, but his temper burned even hotter.

"You are here, my Gypsy, because of my indulgence. Do not forget that. And since we speak of desires, let us talk plainly. You have already made yourself my mistress in name, if not in fact, by living in my house, and your attendance at the Cyprian's Ball will make you much compromised indeed. So do not fool yourself into thinking yourself an innocent who can reclaim her virtue by changing her locale. Desires always have a cost, my dear. And if the price of gaining your brother's respectability is your own, that is a choice you make. So do not throw my generosity back in my face as if I offered you less than nothing."

She stiffened, and for a moment he glared down at her, his jaw clenched, his eyes blazing, heat radiating from him.

His anger provoked a matching one inside Glynis. But in her heart she knew that deep anger always covered a deep hurt. She wanted to lash out because his words stung. And for him to claw at her now meant that she had hurt him.

Ah, but she had thought him invulnerable. A man without a heart. She had feared his power over her, and so she had guarded herself so carefully that she had not given a thought to any harm she might do him. She had scorned him because his offer tempted too much.

But now she saw the glitter in his eyes, and she knew that he did not live above others. He lived apart from them. Ah, but she knew how lonely that was.

Taking his hand in hers, she eased his tight hold from

her chin and lowered his hand. The heat in his eyes softened.

She nodded to herself and lifted her chin. It was as her mother had said—what would be, would be.

"You are right," she said. "It is my choice. So what do you wish me to wear to this Cyprian's Ball?"

EIGHT

Something changed between them. Glynis felt it at once, but she could not name it. That pull she had felt to him intensified, and she could only stare up into his eyes. He stared back, his gaze searching her face, only she did not know what he was looking for.

However, she knew in that instant that if he took her hand now she would go wherever he led.

Ah, but she wanted her arms around him. She ached to hold him, to touch him, to cradle his cheek in her hand, to lie with him. She wanted to ease the loneliness of life for him—and herself.

But it could only lead to heartache. To a parting that must come, for he had no place in her life, and she had none in his. Except for this moment's desire.

And still she wanted it.

But his twisted smile slipped back into place, and his eyelashes, tipped golden at the very ends, lowered to hide whatever lay in those wicked green eyes of his.

Lifting her hand, he kissed the back of it, his lips warm as summer, and then he said, his tone casual, as if nothing had happened, "Why, my dear, you shall go as a Gypsy, of course."

He was mad. And she was mad to follow. Christo told her so. She told herself so. And still she listened to St.

Albans's plans. He had a far more devious mind than either she or Christo. That worried her, but she began to believe that he actually might help them. Or perhaps he was simply helping her down the path toward losing her virtue.

"If you dress as a Gypsy, then Nevin—your pardon, Francis Dawes—cannot help but be interested," St. Albans had said to her. "He will think I am making a private joke of him, which I am. But he will also wonder—and he will want to know for certain—if you are the Gypsy who tried to steal from him. So all we must do is make certain he glimpses you, but that he is left unsure and needing to meet you."

She listened to his words, to his certainty, and she wished she could be as confident as he of how Francis Dawes would react. In truth, she did not know the man, and could not guess his thoughts. He was her blood—her father's brother. But all she could feel for him was a deep hatred. And fear.

What if Francis Dawes recognized her as more than a Gypsy? What if he knew her for his late brother's child, and sent his men after her?

Ah, this seemed such a dangerous scheme. Almost as risky as it was to break into Nevin House to steal the box. They could hang for that.

So she would trust St. Albans a little. At least with him she knew he did not want her dead. He wanted many other things from her, yes, but not that.

Seeming in a mood to be pleased, St. Albans made himself a charming and an affable host. Not even Christo's glowering looks could disturb St. Albans's easy smile. He challenged Christo to cards in the evening, and he took her shopping during the day. He arranged for a dancing master to teach her to waltz, but when he saw how easily she picked up the steps, he swept her around the room, spinning her until she was breathless, his hand firm on the small of her back and pulling her close.

Flushed and too aware of that tug of attraction to his physical grace, she had pulled away. Then she showed him how Gypsies dance—not touching, but with fire in the eyes and in the feet, twirling and lifting her skirts, flirting with every sensual move and twist.

Hunger came into his glance, so hot that it warmed her skin and left her light-headed with the power she had to pull that look from his eyes.

But Christo had come into the room, so St. Albans had done nothing other than watch her.

What would be, would be, she told herself again. *Do not regret what happens, or what does not happen.*

However, she could almost wish that life could go on like this. Pleasant and drifting. Except that her mother and Bado waited. And Christo's temper shortened, and she knew that his restless steps took him too often to Nevin House. He could not live this way forever.

So it was with both relief and cold hands that she stepped into the Argyle Rooms on Regent's Street. Taking a deep breath, she smoothed a hand over the gown that St. Albans had chosen for her. It would amaze her if Francis Dawes recognized her at all, even as a Gypsy.

No Gypsy had ever worn a red gown so dashing, the material impractically thin and cut low with gold coins sewn around the hem and the bodice. She had even bent one coin, just to see if it really was soft gold. It was. The gown was silk, as was her turban, a red-and-gold brocade with fringe that hung down from the side and tickled her bare shoulder, and which made her think that perhaps when she left this would find its way into her things.

Ah, but she should not be thinking of that now.

She was here for a reason.

Only her reason for coming did not seem to be here.

Scanning the room, she stood with St. Albans in the entrance to the main salon. She had not expected such elegance. Tall and rectangular, the long room stretched before her, with carved statues set along the white walls above the doorways that led into other rooms. A small orchestra played at the far end, on a raised platform, while gentlemen in their fine dark coats and evening clothes, and ladies in all manner of dress, danced and talked, laughed and drank.

The men glanced at her, interest and speculation in their eyes. The women also gave her glances, but with hard, jealous eyes. Glynis stared back, a little scornful of these *gadji,* and a little envious of their easy confidence.

A lady dressed as a pageboy danced past, her hair cut short, her slim figure encased in blue velvet breeches that showed her every curve and a tight coat that she filled in a way no boy ever would.

Glynis turned away from the crowd, towards St. Albans. "You said he would be here. Well, where? And how should we ever find him in this crowd, even if he does come?"

"Questions, questions. Always impatient questions. I have said he will be here, and he will. I have arranged it. Now, I shall fetch you champagne to occupy your busy tongue."

Frowning, she glanced around the room again. A woman dressed in a Grecian gown so sheer it might as well not have been there at all, stared at Glynis, her face painted and her expression appraising.

Glynis wished Christo were here. But St. Albans had allowed his presence only if he came with the grooms.

"There are limits to my abilities," he had said. "And while I can make the world believe you are my mistress, no one would mistake your brother for a gentleman."

It was true. Even with his hair cut and his face clean-shaven, and dressed in the earl's black livery, Christo looked more ruffian than either a servant or a gentleman. Glynis would have liked him closer just now, for the stables felt a very long way from these glittering rooms with their bright candles and decadent guests.

St. Albans's arm came around her waist. "Don't worry, my Gypsy. Every man here knows you are under my protection."

"Yes, and the women know it, too, and they do not seem to like it." She slanted a look at him. "You seem to be a great prize, to judge by how they look at me."

His mouth crooked. "How do I answer that? If I say that I am, I sound insufferably conceited. And if I say I am not, then I am lying. However, I think you are the reason for so much notice. I do not make it a habit to keep a mistress. I prefer conquests to liaisons."

She frowned at him. "And what is the difference?"

His amusement deepened. She was, he thought, the most blunt-spoken woman he had ever known. She really should not be asking him these questions. And if she honestly were the daughter of Edward Dawes, she should not be here unless she intended to join these ladies of the town in their profession.

"The difference, my Gypsy, is one of longevity."

"Ah, you mean you tire too easily of these painted ladies. I can see why. They must be performing the entire time they are with you—that is what they are paid for, after all—and it seems to me it would be worse than living with a performing monkey to live with one of them."

His smile widened. That was perhaps the most accurate description he had ever heard for why he did not care to keep a mistress. They were exhausting creatures, but he had assumed that to be because they were women. Well, his Gypsy certainly did not perform for him. That was part of her charm. She was one of the few people he knew who seemed to accept him as he was, neither shunning nor fawning over him.

Offering his arm, he led her to the refreshments and procured her a glass of wine. He pointed out a few notables—Society was starting to thin already as the summer weather began to arrive. In a month, the Thames would begin to stink of sewage, and any who could flee would do so.

He introduced her to a few acquaintances, naming her only as his Gypsy and refusing to tell them anything else about her. He wanted her to seem mysterious, and he could see already that talk had begun to spread. It was going exactly as he knew it would. Now all that needed to happen next was for Duncastle and Hammond—those intimates of Lord Nevin—to play their parts.

The orchestra struck up a waltz, and St. Albans led his Gypsy onto the floor. He swept his arm around her, and her body stiffened as if he had never before held her this intimately.

"You are supposed to look as if you are enjoying yourself—not as if you are enduring the Inquisition," he said, smiling at her.

"I am enduring. It feels . . . well, it feels wicked to have you hold me with so many staring at us."

He pulled her closer. "My dear, a taste for wickedness is like a taste for champagne: it seems bitter and strange at first, and then it goes to your head and you start to wonder how you ever lived without it."

She tilted her head and her eyes narrowed. "Oh? So you were not always wicked?"

"Well, actually I was. But I only managed to excel later in life. It is rather difficult, after all, to be too very wicked when in short pants."

She lowered her stare, but not before he glimpsed the smile in her eyes. In truth, dancing with her was far better than champagne, or any number of the wicked sins that lay on his soul. He liked having her in his arms, her hand resting on his shoulder.

"Now what are you thinking, my Gypsy?"

"It is just another tiresome question."

"I am becoming inured to them. Ask."

"I was wondering if one becomes wicked because of one fateful act that changes one's life, or if it is more like tossing pebbles into a stream. You toss in a few and it does not seem to matter, but if you keep tossing, soon you have dammed the water."

"Dammed. Yes, that sounds more like it. Dammed the water and a life."

"Not your soul?"

"An unseen spirit that abides in the body? I am not certain I have one of those. Perhaps that accounts for my sinful nature."

"Ah, but you must believe in something?"

His gloved hand tightened on hers. "Must I? Then I shall believe in the softness of your body, in the pleasure of a kiss, in what I can hold and touch and see. I can tell you that I believe that nothing lasts forever, so why not enjoy what is here before us now?"

She shook her head, as if she disapproved. "Now you talk like a *gaujo* who lives too much inside a house. You can feel the wind, but you cannot hold it. A soul is like that. And the earth will go on breathing her winds for long after we are gone. That's forever. And if you lie in the woods at night, you would know that spirits are everywhere with us—and you would feel yours rise up to the stars as you lie on the ground, counting their endless number."

The music stopped and St. Albans stilled. Her voice had dropped to a husky, bewitched tone and he could almost wish to carry her off to those woods of hers so they could lie together under the stars, and he would see if he could feel what she had described.

Reality returned as another lady brushed against him, and the orchestra struck up the notes for the next dance.

St. Albans glanced to his right, to the entrance, and saw Lord Nevin talking to Duncastle and Hammond. It seemed they had done as he had known they would and had spread word to Nevin that St. Albans would be sporting a new mistress tonight—a Gypsy.

He smiled. And so it began.

Glancing down at his enchanting Gypsy, regret feathered down his spine. His Gypsy lived in a magical world of luck and spirits, of great love, and lost inheritances that could be found.

What a pity that was not the real world. The reality was that people died too young, and no one particularly cared when they did. Poets wrote of love, but when it came down to it, a woman would choose security instead of a dangerous passion. Greed, lust, and fear drove this world.

But he had not the heart to destroy her illusions tonight.

Life would do that soon enough.

Taking her hand, he led her to the sidelines. "Come, my Gypsy. Your quarry is here, so it is time for you to become one of these performing beauties."

She started to look around her, her gaze searching, but St. Albans kept her moving. "No, do not crane and stare as if you are seeking him. Remember, you do not know this man. He will notice you, and you are to look through him as if he did not exist, and then we shall fade into the crowd and leave him searching."

She forced a stiff smile, but he saw how her face had paled a little. "I wish I knew how you know these things."

"Why, my dear, I am the Earl of St. Albans."

* * *

Christopher waited in the darkness. He had pulled off the white gloves that he was supposed to wear and had tugged loose the white cravat that lay too tight around his neck. Now he lifted a shoulder, uncomfortable in the tight jacket and waistcoat. These *gadje* dressed for looks, not for comfort, more fools them.

He stared up at the lighted windows of the Argyle Rooms. But it was useless. He could see nothing.

He had been watching for the coach with the Nevin crest upon its doors. And he had stood in the shadows as three men had climbed out of the coach and mounted the stairs to be admitted by the porter. His knife had been in his hand, and if it had been only Francis Dawes, he would have thrown the man back in the coach and they would have had a short family reunion.

Very short.

But always the man had someone next to him. It had been like this for all the time they had tracked him. First in the countryside, near the village of Nevin, then on the road to London. Servants surrounded him like lice on a rat. He was, it seemed, a man who could not stand his own company.

Well, he had reason for that.

Frustrated, Christopher turned away and started around the side of the building, to the narrow mews that lay behind and which housed the stables. He could hear the Nevin grooms talking to the other servants, their voices a deep rumble in the night. The air smelled of stables and horses, and he could see the dark coach with its crested doors as it stood on the cobblestones. Grooms threw light blankets over the steaming horses to keep off the evening's chill.

Pausing, Christopher tried to gauge who might be the friendliest of the staff. The short fellow? Or the tall one with the touch of Irish in his voice. Ah, well, he would soon find out.

He gave one last glance up at the windows, where candlelight danced. He did not like Glynis being so close to their uncle tonight. At the inn, their plan had not included even a glimpse of him. Now, here she was, dancing past him in that too-thin gown.

Christopher frowned. If that *gaujo* lord ever hurt her, that one would pay with his blood. That he swore.

However, in a room of people she would be safe enough tonight—both from their uncle and that *gaujo* earl.

Then, with luck, it would not be too much longer before they had the box in their hands. He said a small prayer that their father's box would have the proof they sought.

Putting on a smile, he moved forward, ready to do what he must to make himself friendly. He had dice in his pocket, and a few coins. They would like him well enough if he lost his shillings to them. And he had hidden a bottle of St. Albans's brandy in the Earl's coach. That might also help him loosen some tongues.

But it was going to be hard to joke and laugh with his sister so close to a man who thought nothing of murder.

Francis Dawes stared at the woman in the red gown, frowning, absently listening to Duncastle and Hammond complain of the Select Committee that had been appointed to look into the practice of using boys as chimney sweeps.

"I ask you, what's the world coming to? They have to use boys, for a man won't fit, that's what I say. And what affair is it of the government to look after every urchin on the streets?"

"Quite right. Damn disgrace. Don't you think so, Nevin?"

Rubbing his chest to ease the pressure that had gathered as it did nearly every evening, Nevin glanced at Duncastle. "Disgrace? I'll tell you what is a disgrace—St. Albans. Look at what he's taken up with. Looks foreign. You said she was a Gypsy?"

The last he addressed to Hammond, who lifted a hand, and then brushed the snuff from his dark-blue evening coat. "I didn't say. St. Albans did himself. Said it at White's today. Said he'd found her on the road a few weeks ago."

Uneasy and unsettled, Nevin glanced back to where he had last seen St. Albans. It could not be, he told himself. St. Albans was only attempting to amuse himself with a joke in poor taste.

Pulling out a handkerchief, he dabbed the sweat from his brow. Could no one in London keep a room to a decent temperature? The orchestra had struck up another dance and all he could see were women with gowns cut indecently low and men grinning at them like idiots. The pressure in his chest tightened.

What if it was the same Gypsy?

It would be just like that blackguard St. Albans to take up with some common thief. The man had no morals. No shame. He had run off with a duchess's sister once, and then refused to marry the lady. And that was not the only lady he had ruined. The wine soured in Nevin's mouth as he thought back to the widow Casset, and a wave of queasiness passed over him.

Damn, but that loss still rankled. St. Albans had as good as paid her for her services—giving her money, turning her from respectability, setting her beyond the pale. And beyond his reach. In a better world, a scoundrel such as he would have been shot by a jealous husband years ago.

However, he had Lucifer's luck, and too accurate an aim for anyone to challenge him lightly.

"Where is he now?" Nevin demanded, twisting and pulling at his watch chain. "I want to meet this Gypsy of his."

Hammond, the tallest of the trio, stretched upward. "Isn't that him leaving? Yes, taking his Gypsy with him. I tell you, she looks Italian to me. Said to be quite hot-blooded, those Italian ladies. Wouldn't surprise me at all if that's what she really is. Don't care for those foreigners myself, but you know St. Albans. There is nothing too low for his tastes."

Lord Nevin scowled and glanced around the room, rubbing at his chest again, but now eyeing the women and determined to forget St. Albans and his jokes.

Damn, but it was too much a coincidence. Only why would they resurface now, after twenty years? No, they must be dead, or they had learned their place and now kept to it.

"Gypsies," Nevin muttered, the word sour in his mouth and curling in his stomach like a writhing snake.

"Yes, now there's a Select Committee to start," Duncastle said. "Get rid of these plaguity Gypsy vagabonds. I say, is there anything to drink here, d'you think?"

Nevin scowled. "Oh, I know how to get rid of Gypsies. I know exactly how."

Glynis sat in the corner of the coach, one hand covering her mouth as she yawned.

"Am I boring you?" St. Albans asked.

She shook her head. She could see him only as shadows, but the diamond in his cravat flashed even with the dim light of the coach lanterns.

"I hardly know what I expected," she said. "Something more dramatic, I think."

"I think you expected him to recognize you. I told you he would not. A man who does not wish to see the truth will not. Nevin is a hypocrite—he will not be able to see the truth because he practices deceiving himself."

"How do you know that about him?" she asked.

"Let us just say that we had a brush more than a few years ago over a certain lovely widow. And after being disappointed, Nevin actually thought he could lead Society in cutting my acquaintance. Instead, he made a fool of himself. The earls of St. Albans have put kings on the throne of England, and he thought to challenge me."

She heard the cold satisfaction in his voice and a chill trickled down her back. And curiosity nibbled at her thoughts. If what he had done had displeased Francis Dawes, she wanted to hope that it was something that would please her. But if a woman had been involved—a widow—she was not certain she wanted to hear this story of his.

The carriage stopped and Christo opened the door for them. He handed Glynis out, and then St. Albans stepped out and looked him over. With a shake of his head, he moved away. "And the world calls *me* disreputable."

Worn out by the evening, Glynis wanted only her bed. She had been ready for this night to change her world—only nothing had happened, really. She had thought to face her uncle; she had braced herself for potential disaster, and all her energy had been spent on that.

With a smile she turned to St. Albans. "Thank you."

He glanced at her, surprised and a little wary. "For what, my Gypsy? For a lovely evening?"

"For making it all go exactly as you said it would."

She hesitated, then stood on tiptoe and kissed his cheek. Turning, she ran up the stairs.

St. Albans stood watching her, then he turned and saw his Gypsy's brother watching him, his eyes dark and snapping. He lifted one eyebrow. "Such a pity you are not really my footman. It would give me such great satisfaction to sack you without notice, reference, or pay."

Christo offered an unrepentant grin. "Too bad, *gaujo*. But we shall be gone soon enough." He started up the steps, taking them two at a time, looking light-hearted.

His own mood darkening, St. Albans watched him. This young idiot had taken some scheme into his mind, no doubt of it. He was tempted to allow the fellow to find the hangman in his own fashion. However, his Gypsy would not like that.

And he realized then, with a touch of surprise, that what his Gypsy liked had become important to him.

"Well, what did you find out?" Glynis said, sitting up in her bed, feather pillows plumped behind her and her bare feet tucked under the fine linen sheets.

Eyes alight, Christo gave her a sly smile, then his expression sobered as he perched on the edge of her bed and stared hard at her. His footman's uniform was rumpled almost beyond recognition, with his shirt open, his waistcoat undone, and his coat collar turned up like a highwayman's.

"You first. All went well?" he asked, his tone brusque.

She nodded. "If you call it well to have done no more than to have seen him from across the room. But he saw me. Now St. Albans says he will call. And when he does not see me, he will write and invite me to come to him."

Her stomach tightened and she rubbed cold hands together. "To own the truth, Christo, I was glad not to have to look into his eyes tonight. I am not certain I can do that and not spit in his face."

Christo covered her hands with one of his own. His eyes darkened with a reckless glint that had worry tightening inside Glynis again.

"What? What are you thinking?" she asked.

"That you won't have to face him until after we have the papers in our hands to prove him a liar." He leaned forward. "I learned of another way into Nevin House."

NINE

Glynis pulled her hands from under her brother's touch to fuss with the collar of her high-waisted dressing gown, tugging its velvet edging closer around her bare neck.

"But, Christo, the Earl said—"

"The earl said! What do we care of that *gaujo's* schemes?"

"We care because everything he said would happen tonight, did happen—exactly as he said it would. He knows how Francis Dawes thinks. He knows how to lay traps that neither you nor I could ever build, and he has the power and influence that we lack. If we listen—"

"Listen!" Rising, Christo strode away from the bed. Then he turned, one hand rubbing the back of his neck. "How do we know this *gaujo* is not leading us into one of his traps? One baited with our own desires! He is like the devil, that one. He knows what we most want, and then he smiles and just names the price of your soul for it!"

"Bah! He doesn't even believe in his own soul. What he wants is to make trouble for Nevin."

Christo's hand dropped from his neck. "What he wants is to make you as corrupt as he! He wants you in his bed. And when he has you there, do you think you will come away with no mark upon you? I know you, *phen*. It is not just your body that you will give when you give yourself. But how will you feel after, when he discards everything else you offer?"

Crossing her arms, she hunched one shoulder. "How I feel about anything is my concern."

"And it is mine, as well. If you really wish to jump off a cliff, I cannot keep you from it. But I can warn you of the jagged rocks at the bottom." He came back to her and sat down again on the bed next to her. Her glance slid to where his hand lay, so brown in contrast against the white linen.

She did not want to look into his eyes. She knew all this. She needed no reminder.

"Ah, *phen,* I wish I could tell you to just take your pleasure from him as he wants to take his from you. Some women are made so they can do that—as are some men. But some of us cannot separate our souls from our bodies, and we cannot separate our hearts and our heads. And so what is easy for others becomes something tangled for us."

Gently, he lifted her chin so that she had to look at him. Sadness touched his eyes and his smile. *"Jek rat, jek jakha, jek dji, jek porh, jek bat."*

The Romany phrase echoed in her. *Same blood, same eyes, same soul, same belly, and of one happiness.*

He let go of her chin. "Sometimes you cannot help where fate takes you, but there are heartaches enough in this world without seeking those that can be avoided. You do not have to settle for the little that this *gaujo* has to give you in return for what you can offer him. Wait. Wait for a man who can love you as you deserve."

She stared up into her brother's dark eyes, a hollow ache in her chest. "But what if I cannot love any other?"

He smiled at her. "If you can learn to love one, you can learn to love another."

"Mother never did."

His smile faded, and she was sorry that she had allowed those words to slip out.

Ah, but she did not want to walk in her mother's steps. She did not want to fall in love with a high-born lord. She wanted a simple life. An easy life. Instead, it always felt as if she struggled up a hill that never crested.

Covering her brother's hand with hers, she smiled at him to take away some of the worry her words had caused him. "But we are both talking by moonlight, and you know that *Dej* says that is a time for dreams, not plans. Go to bed, Christo. Tomorrow we'll talk, and make our plans in hard daylight."

He took her hand and squeezed it tight. Then he rose and strode from the room, taking with him his restless soul and his dark moods.

Glynis let out a sigh, then curled up on her side, staring at the candle that burned steady on the table beside her bed. She left the flame aglow. She did not want the darkness tonight. She did not want her thoughts, either, but she could not seem to let go of them as they spun in an endless circle.

Rain began to patter on the window, a soft tapping. The soft rhythm began to soothe her. She could almost imagine it drumming on a tent as she lay on a carpet settled over leaves. Only such a bed was never as soft as this feather one, and a tent was never as warm—as free of drafts—as this lovely room. Ah, but this earl was seducing her, with comforts that he would one day tell her to leave and promises he might not keep. But what else could she do but keep walking the path she had started down?

Slowly, her eyelids became too heavy to hold open. Exhaustion numbed her arms and legs. Her breathing slowed and uneasy dreams claimed her night.

* * *

The drumming changed to hoofbeats—thudding into mud as the horse galloped down the road, its sides wet and hot, its breathing labored. Cold chilled the night, and clouds hid the moon and stars, and the rider's cloak snapped and fluttered like a warrior's banner.

My father is dying, I must get home.

Glynis stirred in her sleep, both saddle-weary and yet not, hunched over her mount's neck, and also hovering above the world, watching with fear tight in her chest.

The rider drew rein momentarily at a crossroad. He lifted his face, considering his choices, and in that instant in the dark, she saw both herself and Christo in the lean, hard profile of Edward Dawes.

Word had come, she knew, by the way that word came to those who traveled the road, from one mouth to the next until it reached the man who needed to hear it.

Lord Nevin is dying.

How long had it been since the argument? Four years? Five? He could not leave that between them. He had to go back, even though the children were babes still. Even though his Anna begged him not to. He had to go back.

And so he rode.

With a troubled sigh, Glynis turned again. Urgency filled her. Anxiety and fear. And she drifted deeper.

Edward burst into the room—his father's room. It was too late. He knew that from the black crepe that hung on the front knocker, limp and dripping from the rain as if even the house mourned the baron's passing. He knew it from the silence in the house and the darkness of his father's chamber, where only a fire burned, its embers red and themselves dying.

His cloak hung limp and wet from his shoulders. His hair lay slick against his head and the rain had chilled him through.

He ought to have come back sooner, and regret lay on him as heavily as his sodden cloak. He strode to the bed and looked down at his father's face, peaceful and pale. He laid his hand over his father's cold one—so much colder than his own.

"I will make you proud of me. And so will my son." The vow came from a voice cracking with emotion, a voice he hardly recognized as his own. But he meant it. He had never intended it to end this way.

Then he turned and saw his brother in the doorway—Francis, his eyes glowing angry and his face livid and red, as if he now stood in place of their father, with his pride and his scorn.

Francis's face darkened. "So, you've a Gypsy bastard?"

Anger flared in Edward. He did not want this again. It had been bad enough with his father, but he would not stand for this from Francis.

"My son is no bastard. I married the woman I love."

"You killed him," Francis said, stabbing a finger towards the still figure on the bed. "For a Gypsy whore."

Two strides and then Francis lay on the floor, his mouth bleeding, and Edward stood over him, rubbing his knuckles. "Don't you ever, ever refer to my wife with anything but respect. I am Lord Nevin now, and she is my lady-wife."

He turned for the door, his cloak swirling around his ankles, those unforgivable words between him and his brother. Francis had never understood. He had always been too like their father—too ready to put himself above the rest of the world. Well, that ended now. His Gypsy wife would bring her laughter into this cold house, and his children would bring their voices and dancing.

Thinking of them, he started down the stairs.

A voice made him stop and turn on the top step.

Francis came forward, the vein on his right temple throbbing. Edward glanced down at the pistol in Francis's quivering hand, then he looked at his brother again.

"You won't shoot me," he said, utterly certain of it. Francis was many things, but he would not shoot his brother.

His face twisting, Francis stopped in front of Edward. "How dare you come back!"

Edward glanced at him, sorry for what he had become. Sorry that their father's rancor had found so ready a home in his brother. He could only shake his head and be grateful that his Anna's love had saved him from that. He did not even recognize in this man the boy who had once tagged at his side.

Well, Francis followed him no longer.

Bitter fury twisted Francis's face. "Get out!"

Turning, Edward started down the stairs.

"Get out!" Francis yelled again.

And then the jarring blow fell on Edward's shoulder as the pistol butt struck him, so strong that it took him off balance, tangling his wet cloak around his feet, tripping him. He clawed for a handhold on the railing but damp fingers slipped. He could not stop himself and the world turned upside down.

Glynis screamed.

She came upright in her bed, shaking, the image of her father's broken body at the base of the stairs lingering, more vivid and real than the darkness around her. Heart still pounding, blood surging in her veins, she drew in a ragged breath and fisted the linens in trembling hands.

The sob came out on its own, shaking and lost.

And then from the darkness, strong arms enfolded her. She let go of the bedding and threw her arms around solid warmth and blessedly strong muscles. Burying her face against warm flesh and soft fabric, she breathed in his scent and tried to blot out the images.

A dream. A nightmare. That was all.

But still her heart raced, and her stomach quivered.

Could it really have happened?

"Oh, God," Glynis murmured, shivering, unable to stop the trembling, ashamed that she could not control herself.

Thankfully, the arms tightened around her, and she clung to them, not caring who held her, but only needing to feel safe. Tears coursed down her cheeks, wild as a flooding river.

"What is it?" St. Albans said, his voice low and harsh, and the now-familiar tone of it soothed her.

She shook her head and simply clung to him, pulling in deep breaths between the sobs.

Impotent fury swept St. Albans, replacing the blind panic that a moment ago had propelled him into her room. He had been awake—as he often was at this hour—nursing a brandy in his own rooms when he had heard that muted cry of utter terror. He had not even paused to fetch his pistol, but went to the secret connecting door between their chambers, cursing himself for misjudging Nevin, certain the fellow had sent someone after her.

Only when he came into her dark room, he saw nothing but her white face, and heard nothing but her sobs.

He shifted on her bed, uncomfortable and with his arms full of weeping woman. What in blazes was he to do with that?

The rain had stopped. Moonlight streamed into the room, bathing it in a pale light that turned the world a bleak silver. She smelled of lavender and an intoxicating musky woman's scent that stirred his body, but he could hardly seduce a woman who quivered in his arms like a wounded bird.

Taking her shoulders, he held her away from him. "What in blazes is wrong?"

She blinked, and glanced around her as if she had been lost somewhere else and had just returned. Then she stiffened, brushed at the wetness on her cheeks, and said, her voice gruff, "Nothing is wrong. Or everything. I don't know."

Her voice quavered on the last words, and he heard the tears she fought to stem.

Irritation with her swept away the last of his fear. He did not like weeping women. And he hated to be clutched at so desperately. That conjured all-too-unpleasant memories of Alaine. How she had clutched at him, and wept after he had bedded her; then he had told her that that was all he had ever wanted from her.

That had been such a lie.

But, God help him, Alaine had lied to him. She had said she loved him. And then she had smiled as she married a duke, as her family wished.

Revulsion sickened him. He had acted an idiot to fancy himself in love with Alaine, and then he damned himself by seducing her. He got what he wanted from her. He had his revenge. And he paid for it with the memory of how she wept in his arms afterwards—her tears and anger and begging, and then, much later, her cold hatred after he seduced her sister.

But those damnable feelings he had thought long buried stirred in their graves again. And he could almost hate his Gypsy for reminding him of the shameful sense that had forever haunted him that he was missing some vital part which everyone else seemed to have.

And his arms quivered with the desire to strike out at something. Because he did not know what else to do.

She wept in his arms, and he did not know how to give comfort, or whatever else it would take to stop her tears. He knew far better, in fact, how to make her cry again. He knew how to look after himself, and that was all he knew.

Well, he did not care. He had already proven to himself, time and again, he was heartless. He might as well prove it to her.

Releasing her, he rose from her bed and stood there, staring down at her. Lord, but she was lovely by moonlight, her skin made pale, her shift slipping off one round shoulder. If he were a gentleman, he would ignore those stirrings of lust that she roused in him. He would leave and allow her time to reassemble her armor. She looked so vulnerable.

Thank Hades and Heaven, he was no gentleman.

"Would you care for a brandy?" he asked.

Biting her lower lip, she hesitated. He could not see her expression clearly, but her eyes glimmered in the moonlight as she stared up at him, and then she nodded.

He was back in a moment with the decanter and two glasses. She sat up in her bed, her dressing gown now wrapped around her shoulders, the room bathed in moonlight. She sat very still, her sobs slowed to occasional sniffs as he poured the brandy. Then she took the glass he offered and held it between both of her hands.

"To fewer dreams," he said, lifting his glass. The crystal rang as he touched the rim of his glass to hers.

She tipped back the brandy in one swallow and then held out her glass for more. This devil's spawn was one of his own kind. Smiling, he obliged.

With another sniff, she gestured with her glass to the secret door that stood exposed against the room's paneling. "I should have expected that."

"And I should have expected this. You dreamed of Nevin, didn't you, after seeing him tonight?"

She nodded again, the darkness of her hair catching a faint glimmer of moonlight. St. Albans stretched himself across her bed, his brandy glass in one hand. "I thought you Gypsies could foretell the future by reading dreams. One of my aunts swore by such nonsense."

"There are those with such a gift. But I dreamed of the past. Of my father's murder."

St. Albans straightened, every muscle tensing and his anger stirring. "Murder? By heavens, if your soul is not as black as my own from your lies, then—"

"What lie?"

"Lies of omission, my dear. You neglected to cover this detail in your earlier renditions of this tale."

"Well, I can hardly tell you the truth when I am not certain of it myself. But what else can anyone think when a young man goes back to a family that hated him, and then is dead within a fortnight's time?"

St. Albans's mouth thinned. He knew quite well what he would think, but he had a naturally suspicious nature. "Tell me about this dream," he ordered.

Glynis told him. She stumbled through the story, tripping over her words in a way he had never heard before. That alone left him uneasy.

What in blazes had happened to Edward Dawes?

What she did not tell him stood out like a light in the room. Her voice quivered at points, and he could imagine what she must have felt. He had had similar dreams as a child, when he had first started to ride, of his own father's fatal fall.

"But it was just a dream," she said, as she finished.

The earl's stare remained on her. Even in the darkness, Glynis felt its intensity. She knew she should not welcome his presence here, in her room, in her bed. But his wide shoulders silhouetted against the window seemed too comforting a reality. She did not want him to go away.

He cursed softly, then said, his voice as hard as icy ground, "What exactly did your mother tell you of your father's death? Did she ever actually accuse Nevin of murder?"

Glynis lifted one shoulder. "For years she said nothing. But I had memories of that night when those men came for us. Something—someone—hunted us. Then, this year, when Christo came of age, she had us sit beside the fire and she told us a *swato* of our father."

She paused and took a long swallow of the brandy, letting its fire burn away the aching cold left by the dream. Somehow it felt right to tell him this. Sitting in the darkness, she knew that she needed to tell someone. Not Christo, for he knew this story already and it troubled him. She needed to talk to someone who had no interest in how her story ended. She needed just to talk.

"My mother said that when my father heard that his father lay dying, he had to go home. She begged him not to. He had fought with his family, and left them to live like a Gypsy. My mother, too, defied her parents, and they never forgave her for marrying a *gaujo*. So they had only each other—and us. But my father would not listen to her. He had to go.

"For a week, my mother waited, each night dreaming of him. And then the dreams stopped, and she could wait no more. Bado had been her friend, so she went to him and left us in his care, and then she went to find her husband."

Pausing, she wet her lips. The old ache rose inside her. The ache for her mother's loss, for her own. Swallowing the tightness in her throat, she went on.

"She found his grave, and servants who talked of how the young lord fell down the stairs the night after his father died. And she heard whispers of an argument. So she went to see his family, to ask them how her husband came to lie in his grave."

"That was not very wise."

"Most likely not. But all she knew was that her husband lay dead, and she did not know why or how. So she went to his family, and she saw his brother laughing with some guests on the drive before Nevin House.

Laughing. He was actually laughing. So she went up to him and cursed him."

Glynis sipped her brandy again, remembering too well how she and Christo had sat silent beside the crackling fire, listening to their mother. She had stared into the fire, her eyes sightless. But Glynis had pictured her mother wild-eyed with grief, cursing Francis Dawes, accusing him of murder before others.

No wonder Dawes had sent men to hunt her down and kill her. He must have feared her as much as he hated her, and her children.

Cloth rustled, then she felt her empty glass lifted from her hands, and she looked up to find St. Albans standing next to the bed. He set the glasses down on the side table. Then he took her shoulders, easily lifting her so that she knelt on the bed before him, her muscles liquid from the brandy.

"I ought to bloody well throttle you!"

She squirmed, but his fingers dug into her, holding her tight, setting her heart pounding. "What? What did I do?"

"You and that imbecile brother! What in blazes were you thinking not to mention to me that you suspected Dawes of bloody murder before you allowed me to parade you before him like a dove set loose before a hawk?"

Annoyed by his anger, she stopped struggling and gave a derisive snort. "A dove, am I? Yes, I am so helpless, I could not talk you out of your clothes, and could not leave Francis Dawes looking a fool for chasing a phantom Gypsy! I look after myself, *gaujo!*"

Turning, he pushed her onto her back. She tried to roll away, but he loomed over her. His hands found her shoulders again and pinned her to the feather mattress, so that its softness cocooned her, making it impossible to do more than writhe under his grip.

Teeth clenched, she glared at him, her breathing rapid. She wished she had kept his pistol closer. It did little good under the bed where she had left it.

He lowered his face to hers, so that in the moonlight, she could see the glimmer in his eyes, and the hard set to his mouth. Brandy fumes and his own male scent left her head spinning. Fear fluttered in her stomach—and something else as well.

Ah, but she had gotten too comfortable with this one. One might tame a wolf, but that did not make it stop wanting to eat rabbits.

"You are a clever girl, I grant. But desperate men take desperate measures, my sweets. And I would regret losing you before we have a chance to finish what is between us. So from this point on, you will have a touch more care for this skin of yours."

She glared at him, wishing that he could better see the defiance that simmered inside her. *Go ahead, kiss me, gaujo,* she thought, arms tensing to fight him. *You will soon learn that even a rabbit has teeth!*

As she expected, he lowered his mouth to hers. His breath brushed warm on her lips. And then his head bent and he pressed his lips to the hollow of her throat where her pulse hammered.

Liquid heat pooled inside her. Her breath caught in her chest. Her fists tightened as she fought that treacherous ache of desire. She bit down on her own lip, fighting to hold within the sigh that ached for release. Twisting underneath him only made it worse, for it turned that burning touch into a teasing caress of lips and teeth and tongue.

Her muscles slackened. She shut her eyes tight and tried to pretend this was not happening to her, but still her body betrayed her as it sang with joy at his touch.

Lifting his head, he shadowed her again as he rose

over her. She braced herself for worse. Ah, but she should not have trusted this one.

But then he released her and stood. She sat up, rubbing her wrists, glaring at him, wondering if she could reach his pistol before he could grab her again. Ah, but what would that solve? He would smile at her in that infuriating way he did, as if he knew her every thought. And he would go away, only to come back to torment her again.

Scrambling for the edge of the bed, she thumped her bare feet onto the thick carpet and then dragged the dressing gown from her body so that she stood only in moonlight and her nightdress.

"You want to settle what is between us? Well, settle it. You want my body? Go ahead. Take it! Let us have done with this, for that is all you will ever have from me!"

He stood very still for a moment, and then came closer. His stare swept over her, and then he smiled.

"You raise the stakes again, my Gypsy. For I now want far more than your body. Far, far more."

Her mouth went dry.

"Go back to bed." Leaning close, he whispered in her ear, his voice whisper soft, "And dream of all the things I will ask from you one day."

He left her then. Left her standing in her room, her arms bare and cold, her shift feeling transparent, and torn between a desire to throw something at him, a numbing relief, and an odd disappointment. Like a phantom, he disappeared into the dark hole and that secret door clicked shut and vanished back into the room's paneling.

A sudden heat flared in her. She almost wanted to scream again and have him back here to finish this. He wanted more! Bah! He wanted whatever he thought he could not have, and when he had her heart he would look at it and decide he did not want it after all. She knew his kind too well.

Turning, she glanced around the room, and then began to drag a round table carved with exotic fish in front of that cursed door. When she finished, she pushed back the hair that curled around her damp brow. Her shoulders sagged.

She put a hand up to her neck, to the spot he had kissed, and still she could feel how warm his lips had been, and that longing he had stirred within her began to stir again.

Ah, but she did not know who really was more dangerous, or who was her greater enemy—this *gaujo,* or Francis Dawes.

Glynis woke to a bustling in her room. She pried open sleep-weighted eyes, and realized that she had fallen asleep in her dressing gown, curled up in a chair in the salon and not in her bedchamber.

The maid—wide-eyed with curiosity, but seeming too well-trained to say anything about Glynis's choice of bed—dropped her a curtsy, and then asked the question she asked every morning. Would miss prefer tea or hot chocolate?

Glynis asked for tea, and then frowned at the trunks laid open on the floor. "What is this?"

"The Earl wants you ready to leave, miss. Soon as you've had your breakfast."

TEN

A weight settled in the pit of Glynis's stomach. So it had happened. Despite his words and actions of last night, the inevitable had occurred. He had grown tired of her. He had probably gone away angry with her, and had decided this morning that he had had enough of her difficult ways.

She rose, her chin high, telling herself it was for the best. She and Christo would manage without the Earl's help.

Still, it stung her pride. She felt angry with herself that it did so. And that, she told herself, was all she felt.

She dressed quickly in her blue gown, throwing her few things into a bundle that she hastily tied. Reluctantly, she left the fringed turban behind. She could not afford reminders of him.

Then she started down the stairs.

St. Albans stood in the main hall, talking to Gascoyne. As Glynis came down the stairs, St. Albans glanced up at her, dismissed his servant, and then moved to the base of the stairs to wait for her.

His Gypsy, St. Albans decided, looked to be in a decidedly thorny mood. Ashamed perhaps of last night? Head high, dark eyes snapping, she wore that confounded blue gown of hers, her cloak draped over her shoulders. Someday he would really have to burn that rag.

Clutching a small, dark bundle, she stopped before him. "I am ready to go. Where is Christo?"

Still weighing her mood, St. Albans offered a smile. "He is staying behind on this excursion. It is just the two of us."

Shock widened her eyes and she glanced at him, a frown pulling her dark brows together. He realized then what it was. She had mistaken the intent behind his orders. "You thought you were being given your *congé.*"

"My what?" she said, still sounding indignant.

"Your permission to depart," he said, then offered his arm. "You are departing, but with my escort. I want you out of Nevin's reach for a time."

"But why? This is not what you promised! You said you would arrange that I—"

"Plans have changed. No, do not lose your temper just yet. You do have a choice in this—you may stay here, locked in your room, or you may come with me."

"And why should I wish to go anywhere else with you?"

"Because I am curious about this story you have told. Curious enough to have your favorite item—questions. I think you might find the answers interesting. Now, do you come with me, or stay?"

She did not like her choices. He saw that at once, but her preferences did not matter. He wanted her away from Lord Nevin's reach for a time—enough time to make him forget her presence, in fact. And this was not an errand for a servant. Too many nuances might be uncovered, and it was a delicate thing to inquire if the current Lord Nevin might have caused his elder brother's death. That demanded discretion.

So he would have to go, because he hated puzzles, and he had done nothing last night but puzzle over the question of whether his Gypsy could really be telling the truth.

Curse as he might want to, he could not avoid the fact that she had infected him with this quest of hers. At least he had her brother safe under lock and key, where the fellow would not cause further problems. Gascoyne would see to that.

He offered his arm again. "Shall we?"

They covered nearly a hundred and thirty miles in just over ten hours. A reasonable pace, St. Albans thought, but Glynis sat bolt upright across from him the entire time, clasping the strap inside the carriage, declaring that his coachman would overturn them at this speed.

But no such delay overtook them. No horse went lame—St. Albans kept his own horses along each of the major roads, and he changed teams every fifteen miles to keep the pace he liked. No axle broke. No wheel came off. His staff knew how to maintain a carriage.

He could not draw his Gypsy into conversation, and she glared at him if he even leaned towards her, so he left her to her own thoughts and amused himself with a deck of cards and a traveling card table.

At six that evening, with a good amount of light still left in the sky, his carriage pulled up before a snug brick house, not five miles from Nevin, and St. Albans swung out and then turned to reach for his Gypsy.

On solid ground, Glynis eyed the house with misgivings, although its age-yellowed stone facing, its flight of shallow steps that led to the main double doors, and its tidy size and gardens, made an inviting setting. Particularly after ten hours in a swaying coach. Ah, but she felt as if she were still moving.

A wooded hill rose behind the house, as appealing as any home to Glynis and lit with the golden light of a clear blue evening sky.

"Where are we?" she asked.

"Owlpen Manor. One of my lesser holdings. I sent a messenger ahead to have all ready for us. You will want to bathe and change. We dine at eight with the Vicar of Nevin."

She glanced at him. "But why?"

"Because, my sweets, you are now Miss Dawes, and a distant connection of mine. You have an interest in your family history, and a desire to bestow a gift upon the parish in exchange for a glimpse of its records." His smile widened. "You see, you are not the only one who can invent a good *swato.*"

Dinner seemed to Glynis to drag on forever.

She had dressed in a gown of gold silk which had a half-robe of red velvet. She plucked at the velvet, self-conscious, feeling overdressed and out of place. St. Albans acted as if she honestly were a lady, deferring to her every preference, and lightly wielding that devastating charm of his on both her and their host.

The vicar, Mr. Ambrose Cook—a solemn man, gray-haired, and round of figure and face—had greeted them at the Rectory with more caution than hospitality. Glynis realized that he must be aware of St. Albans's notoriety, for the man could not have been more guarded if he were greeting the devil himself.

Still, he offered the earl the deference due his position. After serving them sherry in the drawing room—and after being handed a discreetly proffered check drawn, as the earl said, on his own bank on behalf of Miss Dawes—the vicar's starched formality began to thaw.

Not another word was mentioned by the Earl of why they were there. Not as the vicar took them into dinner. Not as a meal of more pies and sauces and dishes than Glynis could count was laid before them. Not as she retired—as a lady must—to leave the gentlemen to their port, with their promise not to linger.

The housekeeper took Glynis to a retiring room to

answer nature's demands, and to freshen herself. And when she came back to the snug, book-lined parlor, it seemed to her that St. Albans had made himself fastest of friends with the vicar.

Ah, but that man could charm. He would be a wonder at a horse fair.

"Bless me, but do you mean to say you were up at Cambridge with Terrance Hale?" the vicar asked, beaming. "Why, his *Botanical Gardens* sits upon my very shelf here. Have you actually been to his home, to see his gardens, I mean? I have promised myself to make that pilgrimage, but have yet to tear myself from my own tidy plot here."

"Yes, I have been many times," St. Albans said, a slight drawl in his tone. "Shall I ask Tuffy to send you some rose cuttings? They are some of the most glorious in the country."

Glynis sat down and listened to the Earl of St. Albans talk roses. He actually seemed to know of what he spoke, for he and the vicar were soon off into talk of cuttings and mulch, colors and pruning, and things that seemed in another language.

She tried to picture the Earl in a rose garden, perhaps with his coat off, his shirt cuffed. The image had her smiling, but she thought it more likely that he had an army of gardeners and commanded them like a general.

A shadow fell over her and she looked up into the Earl's handsome face. "Have we managed to bore you utterly?"

She glanced around and saw that they were alone.

"Mr. Cook has gone to fetch the rectory keys to take us into the church vaults," St. Albans said, offering her his hand. "Do remember that it is a cousin's wedding you wish to find."

She nodded and rose. Then she glanced at him. "Do you really grow roses?"

"A sensualist ought to indulge his senses—all of them," he said, and then his eyes lit. He lifted her bare hand to his lips, for she had taken off her gloves in the retiring room. "Sight we take for granted. But that is just the starting point."

His lips brushed the back of her hand. "There is touch."

His tongue teased her skin with a soft feathering, and then he lifted his mouth. "Taste."

She stiffened and tried to glare at him. "Do you not recall that Mr. Cook is supposed to think me the respectable Miss Dawes tonight?"

His eyes gleamed wicked, delighting in it. "That certainly covers hearing, although those were not quite dulcet tones. But we cannot overlook scent—it is a woman's scent that lingers most in a man's mind."

Still holding her hand, he lifted it and then breathed deeply, as if taking snuff from her wrist. "A clean smell of soap and rosewater. A pragmatic aroma for Miss Dawes. But you ought to have your own scent, my Gypsy. Something unique. Exotic."

Despite the cooling evening, her neck warmed. "You are trying to flatter me."

"And I am succeeding. Shall I mix you a scent? It is a hobby of mine to do so."

She started to answer him that she wanted no such thing, but Mr. Cook came back into the room, huffing, a sheen on his round face from his search for his keys. He urged Glynis to bring a shawl, warning her that he would not want her to take a chill from the night air.

Ah, if he only knew how many nights I slept in the open. And then she caught a glimpse of the wry amusement in St. Albans's eyes, and she had to look away for she knew that he held the same thought.

St. Albans offered her his arm for the walk, and the vicar chatted about the history of the village—its establishment as a Norman holding near the Welsh border—and the illustrious Dawes family.

"How long have you been vicar hereabout?" St. Albans asked, drawling the question with casual boredom.

Glynis tensed. Could this man have actually married her parents? His answer disappointed.

"Nearly two decades. Yes, a goodly time. Lord Nevin gave me the living after Mr. Allnut—the previous vicar, bless him—left for India. Missionary work, I think it was."

"You never asked him?" St. Albans said, stopping outside the church.

Mr. Cook lifted his lantern and paused, the iron ring of keys jangling softly in his hand. "Never met the man. He left just after the fire that took the old Rectory. No one died, bless us. But I have heard that it broke the man to have had his personal papers burnt. All of them—diaries, letters, books. Thankfully, the parish records have always been kept in the vault. Do go in. The church is always open, and it is only the vault that is kept under lock."

St. Albans opened the door, and Glynis stepped into the church, a little nervous to walk where once her parents had given their vows. She waited a moment for the vicar to enter with his lantern, and then for some sense of recognition of the place. But it was simply a church, not unlike others she had seen.

Stone walls were hung with tapestry, and wooden pews lined the floor. It seemed quite sparse, but she liked the sense of peace that lay within the silence.

Leading the way, the vicar took them to a wooden door that lay to the side. It took him two tries to find the right key, and a good twist to unlock the door, which squeaked on its hinges, proclaiming how rarely anyone entered. A twisted stair of stone steps, worn by footfalls in the middle, led down one flight. Even Glynis had to hunch under the low ceiling.

The vault seemed more storeroom than anything else, lined as it was with wine racks and dusty bookshelves, with a rough-hewn wooden table in the center.

"Bless me now, which year would you care to see?" the vicar asked, setting down his lantern and turning up the wick.

Glynis silently counted back her own age, plus the year in addition that would set the date. "Seventeen-ninety-two. June, please."

Mr. Cook began to search the shelves and Glynis edged closer to the Earl to whisper, "You heard him—a convenient fire, the old vicar gone. We always knew there would be nothing here to find."

St. Albans lifted a skeptical eyebrow and gave her a cool stare. "Ah, but the right nothing can be as revealing as something."

Glynis frowned at him. And then she realized that he was referring to the fact that if they did find the parish register, but did not find her parents' signatures in it, it would prove that no marriage had taken place.

She pulled her shawl a little tighter around her shoulders.

"Ah, here we have it," the vicar said, pulling out a dusty, leather-bound book that was almost too large to manage. He laid the register upon the worktable, and then opened it and stepped back. "What name did you say you were searching for?"

"Edward Dawes," Glynis said.

Mr. Cook frowned. "What? Not the late baron's eldest? Oh, no. You must be mistaken. He never married. Died young, bless him. Tragic accident, I heard."

St. Albans stepped forward. "Quite. But Miss Dawes is recalling a cousin, I believe. Miss Dawes?"

With a nervous glance at the Earl, Glynis came forward and began to scan the parish register as the vicar chattered about the various members of the Dawes family whom he personally knew.

She did not listen, but looked at the names, so carefully inscribed by each couple who had married here. Christian names, middle names, given names. Men and women who had pledged their lives to each other. Were some of them now dead? Some with grown children, and grandchildren even? Some perhaps still living in this area, and who had known her father?

She turned the page, and the date jumped suddenly to October. Her hands chilled. She turned the page back, and then forward and back again, searching for her parents' names. Dear God, had St. Albans been right after all? Was the inheritance she had dreamed of nothing more, really, than her mother's desire for revenge against Francis Dawes?

Ah, but that could not be. It must not be.

Not knowing what else to do, she glanced towards St. Albans.

He stepped closer, then he put a palm on each side of the book, pressing it flat.

There, in the center, she saw it. A sharp edge of vellum that stood up. She ran her fingers down the center of the book, along the edge. And then she looked at the dates that jumped so quickly from June to October.

St. Albans closed the book and turned to the vicar. "It is as we thought—not here."

"I am sorry. Would you care to look at another year? No? Well, then, come back to the Rectory and we shall have some tea before you leave. And if there is any light, you must let me walk you though my gardens. They are quite modest, but I would be interested in your opinion of my *Comte de Chambord,* which has just begun to bud."

The vicar spoke as he put away the book and led them

up the curved stone stairs again. Glynis allowed St. Albans to walk ahead with Mr. Cook; she held back from them, her thoughts dark and her mood even darker.

Someone had cut a page from the register. Someone who had, no doubt, burned the previous vicar's papers, just in case he had a letter or had made a journal entry. But it was negative proof—and nothing to take before the law.

She could almost growl from the frustration of it.

Outside the church, Mr. Cook veered off the path, leading them to the gardens at the back of the Rectory. Glynis allowed the gentlemen to outpace her. St. Albans glanced back at her, his eyebrows lifted in a silent question.

She waved him on. She needed a moment to herself. A moment to mourn the hopes that she had not even realized had risen in her. A moment for a personal visit before they departed.

The vicar's droning voice faded, and Glynis turned her steps towards the quiet of the cemetery.

She walked steadily, peering at the white granite headstones. The sun had set, but the last twilight lingered in the sky with the promise that soon the longest day would be here. The moon had risen full and lush, brighter even than the vicar's lantern.

And then she glimpsed what she sought.

Edward Dawes.

Just his name. Nothing more carved on the headstone. Not a mark that he had been only twenty-nine when he died. Not a mention that he was a beloved father and husband.

Stooping beside the headstone, she brushed her fingers across the cold, hard lettering.

And then a deep voice startled her. " 'Some shape of beauty moves away the pall, from our dark spirits . . .' "

Glynis spun on her heel, lost her balance, and sat

down in the grass. A shadow loomed over her, dark and broad-shouldered, but the man offered his hand and an easy grin.

"I am terribly sorry. I did not mean to frighten you. My father swears I have a scholar's mind and no manners to my life, but I may at least atone for startling you with poetry. Though Keats ought not to startle."

He lifted her to her feet she brushed at her skirts and then looked up at him. "Keats?"

"A poet. A gifted fellow, unlike your humble servant." He swept her a bow. "But what is a lady such as you, 'rich with a sprinkling of fair musk-rose blooms . . .' doing in a graveyard by moonlight? I am quoting at you, and it is very rude of me to do that and not introduce myself. Forgive me, I'm Bryn Dawes. And you are . . . ?"

She stiffened. A Dawes. What would she say to him? She peered closer at his face, but it was too dark to see more than that he was tall, and his voice flowed like a songbird who would not stop singing.

"I am just a visitor," she said. "Now you must pardon me. My host will be wondering where I am."

She started for the Rectory, but he fell into step with her, matching his longer stride to hers. She saw moonlight glance off riding boots.

"So you are visiting Mr. Cook. It's terribly rude of me to pry, I know, but I must ask. Please tell me that you did not come with the Earl of St. Albans."

She stopped and turned towards him. "How did you know?"

"A coach, a crest, they are easy things to see. And in a village this small, difficult to overlook."

"Do you know the Earl?" she asked. His answer would tell much about him, she decided.

He paused a moment, as if weighing his words. "By reputation only. And now I shall be an utter knave and ask if you are safe in his company. Forgive me, if you are. I have this lamentable tendency to insert myself where I am not wanted, but a lady met by moonlight must be a forgiving sort."

She stood there, twisting the ends of her shawl. Ah, what should she say to him? No, I do not want to be here with the Earl? And what would he do? Rescue her? Take her with him? As if she would be safer with a Dawes than with the Earl.

"There is nothing to forgive. But thank you for your concern." She started to walk away from him again.

He hurried to keep pace with her. "Please, I have this sense that I know you from somewhere. Do I? Or is it my uncle whom you knew? That was his grave, was it not?"

Stopping, she turned towards him. "Your uncle? Your father is Francis Dawes?"

Even in the moonlight, she saw his mouth twist. "Yes, I am Lord Nevin's son, and the way you say his name I take it that you are not among his admirers. Please tell me that you are not yet another relative he has offended. Or someone he has wronged. 'Of noble natures, of the gloomy days, of all the unhealthy and o'er-darkened ways . . . ' I am afraid that he does things from the certainty he knows best for all, and he is too often right for his own good. And for the rest of us as well. And here I am babbling and not letting you speak—I do know you from somewhere."

Head spinning, she could only frown at him. He was her cousin. *Jek rat.* Same blood. The tug of kinship lay between them, and he felt it as well to be so certain that he knew her. Blood called to blood, and she saw in the shape of this man the shape of her brother.

But she did not want to know him, or like him. Low, melodic voices, she had learned from the Earl, could too easily beguile.

"I must go."

She started forward, but he called out to her again, so that she paused and turned to him.

He came towards her, fishing in his pockets for something. "Here. Take this. No, no, it is nothing. Merely my card. I cannot rid myself of the feeling that if you travel with the Earl of St. Albans, you travel with trouble. It is the moonlight, I think. Or the graveyard. 'A poor, weak, palsy-stricken, churchyard thing.' But if you have my card, I will know at least that I have offered help."

"Why should you want to befriend me? A stranger."

" 'Mortality weights heavily on me like unwilling sleep.' I have a heavy soul, lady. And I know but one way to lighten it, and that is by aiding others. But it is easy to promise a stranger aid. They so rarely take it."

He took her hand, pressed his card into it, and then bowed low, the courtly gesture oddly touching. "I think you will remember a madman who quoted poetry at you and asked only your name. But I vow I do know you from somewhere. Perhaps someday you will tell me from whence. And I do hope you know the Earl as well as you know my father—both men deserve a good deal of cautious respect."

"What if we never meet again?"

"Oh, we shall meet. I can feel it. And the things I feel in my bones come true. My mother was Welsh, you see. It irritates my father no end that it was so, but she was very rich, and he could not refuse her family's money. And here I am again, talking to you as if you were family."

His grin flashed in the darkness.

She glanced down at his card, a white rectangle in the moonlight. Somehow it gave her reassurance to have it— as if he might be a friend to her. But he might as easily turn from her once he knew her identity. He might prove his father's son.

"Thank you," she said, and then started back towards the Rectory. She stopped once and turned back and saw his dark silhouette. Then she called out, "Glynis. My name is Glynis."

Turning away again, unsettled, she strode back to the Rectory.

She remained silent on the drive back to Owlpen Manor. Thankfully, the Earl did not question her, nor did he try to flatter or flirt. He simply sat next to her in the carriage, his shoulder brushing hers as the coach rocked.

At Owlpen, he handed her from the coach. She felt his stare as he escorted her inside.

"I . . . I am tired. Do excuse me," she said, and then turned and fled up the stairs.

She did not want to face him tonight. She could not. Disappointment lay hollow inside her, and she wanted to be alone.

Ah, what she really wanted was this done and over. If not for Christo, she would flee back to the woods. But it was too late for that escape. She could feel already that life was slipping away from her control.

She thought back to her cousin, Bryn. He had what Christo wanted, and yet he seemed no more content than was her brother. Was no one ever happy with their lives? And here was the Earl, who wanted to make her life yet more complicated.

She could almost wish them all gone, and her life so much simpler.

But what would she do without Christo? Without her *dej*? She needed friend and family, just as she needed air and water.

She allowed the maid to take down her hair, but then dismissed her. When the maid left, Glynis carefully searched the room for any possible hidden panels. She did not want another surprise visit from the Earl. Satisfied at last, she locked the door, and then, still in her evening gown but now barefooted, she opened the window and curled up on a chair.

The night smelled of summer and the breeze touched her face with a mix of summer warmth and cool darkness. Crickets chirped, and an owl called out its warning that it hunted by moonlight. It would be a good night to lie under the stars, the earth at her back. Ah, perhaps she felt unsettled because she had been too long in houses. Perhaps she needed dirt under her feet and wind in her hair.

With a sigh, she settled deeper in her chair, too tired to answer the night's call. Perhaps tomorrow.

Tomorrow.

And then a scrabbling outside her window roused her. Someone was climbing the walls. For a moment, she could only fear that somehow she had betrayed herself with Bryn Dawes, and that, like his father, he had sent someone after her. An instant's fear ran through her, cold as winter.

Could she slip to the window and slam the sill down? Her locked door effectively held her prisoner, for she could not imagine finding the key and turning the bolt while this intruder waited for her.

Heart hammering, she rose and softly padded to her bed, her stare fixed on the moonlit window. Her hand fumbled in the bed linens and then her fingers brushed the cool, hard touch of the pistol St. Albans had given her.

Slipping it out, she pointed it with both hands towards the open window. If it was someone sent after her, she would soon find out. And she would discover as well if she had the fortitude to shoot a man.

ELEVEN

A man's hand, pale-skinned in the moonlight, clamped onto the windowsill. Arms aching, Glynis swallowed the tightness in her throat and wet her lips.

"Hold there! I have a pistol," she called out, grimly determined to shoot if she must.

A muffled voice answered, strained with the effort of clinging to the stone. *"Nais tuke, phen.* Your hand would be of more help."

"Christo?" Lowering the pistol, she stared at the window a moment. How had he found her? What was he even doing here, climbing into her window? With questions buzzing and her blood still racing, she set the pistol on the bed, and then went to the window and glared down at him.

"Why can you not ever use a door like the rest of the world?"

His grin flashed in the darkness. Hatless, he dangled from her window, his booted feet tucked into the grooves between the stone facing. "You want the Earl to lock me up in this house as well?"

Her eyes widened, then her fists clenched. Ah, but she ought to have known that it was St. Albans's idea that Christo stay in London.

Grabbing his arm, she pulled.

He lifted himself up and swung a leg over the windowsill, then let out a deep breath and rested there, one leg still dangling outside. "This one is easier than that house in London, or perhaps it is just that I am getting better at this."

"That, I do not care about. Tell me about London. What happened? How did you find me?"

He grinned again, and then lifted a soft bag from his shoulder and swung into the room. Glynis moved to lay wood on the dying fire, then lit a split of wood and moved to touch the flame to the candles that had been snuffed earlier.

"Find you? How could I not? The Earl's servant—the one who dresses so pretty—could not wait to tell me everything after I sliced the buttons off his waistcoat."

Turning, she frowned at her brother, a faint guilt worming loose inside her. "Ah, poor Gascoyne. He must wish his master had never seen us. I took a pistol to him when he tried to burn my dress."

Christo gave a low chuckle, then sprawled in the chair nearest the fire as if bone-weary. Dust coated his soft boots and his dark clothing. Firelight glinted in his wind-blown hair, and the dark stubble of his beard shadowed his lean cheeks. However, an inner fire lit his eyes with bright excitement.

"Poor Gascoyne! Poor nothing. That one thought he could keep me caged like a tame bear—as if locks and I are not old friends. But I will say this for that *gaujo* of yours—his horse is one a man should never sell. That one has wings."

She tossed the split of wood onto the crackling fire, and then turned to Christo. "You stole the Earl of St. Albans's horse? You really do want to hang."

"Just borrowed. After all, he is in his master's stable again." He sat up then and held out the bag. "But do you not want to know what else I brought with me from London?"

He grinned, then reached into the cloth bag and pulled

out an oblong box. Glynis's heart skipped as she recognized the Dawes dragon carved into the rosewood. Iron hinges and an iron lock gleamed dully in the firelight.

Her jaw slackened. She had seen the box but once, at the Red Lion Inn, although her mother had described it in detail. It was her father's treasure box.

St. Albans tossed back his third brandy and then moved to the decanter in his bedchamber to pour a fourth. He could not please himself tonight. Nothing attracted—not books, not letters with estate business, not anything in his bedchamber.

A silk paisley dressing gown lay over his open-necked shirt, and he still wore his black pantaloons. He did not want to undress for his own empty bed. He had discarded his waistcoat and cravat onto the floor, and his black slippers made no sound as he paced back to the window.

Was it the full moon that made everything but restlessness impossible?

Damn, but he ought to have taken his Gypsy when she offered herself. However, even in that dimly lit room, he had known that she had taken on a martyr's resignation. That was not the emotion he wanted from her.

And then tonight! Tonight her mind had been anyplace but with him. He had charmed. He had offered understanding for her silence. He had taken her to a bloody rectory, for love of heaven, and had looked through appallingly dusty records.

For what?

For a polite good night, with her stare absent and frowning as she turned and left him in his own hall.

Blazes, but he ought to leave her to her virtue. She was a stubborn, willfully independent Gypsy. She asked too many questions, mistrusted his flattery, and tackled her meals with an unladylike gusto.

He frowned into his brandy.

And everything he knew of her spoke of a passion for life that he envied. Far more than he wanted her body, he wanted to wrap himself in that passion of hers with a near-desperate longing.

He sipped his brandy, savoring the complex aroma and the oak-flavored tang, hoping it would numb these insistent urges. They did not serve his plan, and so they really had to be subdued.

If only those wretched records had shown clearly that no marriage had taken place. If only there had not been any evidence of tampering. But it had cast damning suspicion that someone wanted a legal marriage obliterated.

What would he do with her if she proved she was indeed a lady born? Such a detail had never before stopped him from his pleasure. But those ladies had all been willing victims—even the ones who protested. Some—such as Alaine's sister—had thought to trade virtue for marriage, and they had learned better than to try to bargain with a devil such as him. Some had thought only of the delight of sin to be had from a man who had made a career of it.

But his Gypsy wanted only a peaceful cottage in a respectable village.

He let out a breath, disgusted with such an idea. He would give her a month—no, a fortnight—before she found herself bored into purgatory. She was not made for such a pastoral setting, no matter what she thought she wanted.

And it all came back again to the need to prove to her that what she wanted was not what she needed. She needed him, damn all. And he was going to get her to admit it.

He began to smile.

Yes, he would have her admit it. He would have her

surrender that pride of hers to him. He would coax her, and please her, and make it impossible for her to leave.

In fact, he would start tonight. He would give in to these soft urges to go to her, to gather her in his arms and simply hold her. His instincts had not failed him. No, the more he thought on it, the more he realized that that was the approach needed to get what he wanted from her.

A kind word, a shoulder to lean upon tonight——that would weave subtle ties between them before she even knew he had spun his web.

Yes, he liked this new plan—for that's what it was. A plan, not an aching need.

Putting down his brandy glass, he set out for her room.

No doubt she had locked herself in. His smile twisted. He would wager she had also scrutinized every inch of her room as well for other entrances. But he had an ace. His hand slipped into his pocket and tightened around the iron key.

He would give her five minutes to be angry with him, and then he would tell her how he could not sleep. They would talk of the missing page in the register, he would express new belief in her story, and she would soften.

And before this week was out, he would possess her heart as well as her body. By all that was unholy, he would.

Glynis had to sit down. She did so, her knees almost buckling as if someone had struck the back of her legs with a wooden beam. Her hand rose to her throat. Then she looked into her brother's eyes.

"How did . . . If you broke into Nevin House without me, I shall—"

"As if I cannot do anything without my big sister to

guide me. You may be three years older, *phen,* but there are some things that are a man's work."

Her eyes narrowed, but he grinned at that, looking pleased to have gotten the best of her.

"If you do not tell me what you did, I shall curse you with boils that will keep you forever off any horse's back!"

His grin widened. "Keep your curses. I told you I knew another way in—through the servant's door."

He began to talk, boyishly eager, proud of himself, and the knot in Glynis's chest began to unwind. She had thought herself so vital to this task, but it had obviously proven easier for him when he was not burdened with her.

He told the story quickly. As soon as he was free of the Earl's house, he made his way to the stables in the mews behind, looking for a mount to liberate. Before he reached them, he met up with one of Nevin's servants.

"What was he doing at Winters House?" Glynis asked, frowning.

Christo's smile hardened. "Watching. So he could take back word of when you returned. I have no love for that *gaujo*-earl, but he was not wrong to take you from London when he did."

She wrinkled her nose and waved away such a concern, but the thought of someone watching for her return left her uneasy.

Pushing the feeling away, she folded her hands and leaned forward. "But never tell me this servant just let you into Nevin House?"

Christo leaned back in his chair, the box balanced on his lap. He seemed so casual about it, but Glynis could sense his possessive satisfaction in having it within easy reach.

"He did after I told him I had been dismissed by the Earl, and that if I could pay him back with any harm, I would. It works well to speak the truth, you see. The fellow told me I could pay back the Earl. But, of course, I made him dangle some coins to get me to go with him."

"And he took you to Lord Nevin himself?"

Christo's face twisted with scorn. "As if the great man would see me. No, he took me to some grim-faced fellow. A butler, I think. But they liked my stories well enough." He grinned again. "I made you a hired actress who has a terrible temper. And then they had to carry my tale to their master, and that left me alone just long enough."

He spread his hand over the box. "He had it in his study, with his own papers stuffed in the top, as if this was as rightfully his as everything he holds!"

Glynis's stare lowered to the box. For nearly four months now they had plotted to get this prize. Handed down from father to eldest son for five hundred years, this box had kept their father's treasures. Or so their mother had said that he had told her. They had gone to the village of Nevin, to the Dawes country estate, and there they had learned from the servants—a superstitious lot who liked to have their fortunes told—that Francis Dawes always kept this box with him.

Almost as if he knew what it held.

Or as if, for him, it gave him a rightful claim to the title that was not his.

She looked up at Christo, her skin tingling and her pulse beating faster. "Well? Where are the marriage papers?"

He shook his head, his expression turning sullen. "I picked the lock, but there's only our uncle's papers and some stray bits he kept there—a miniature of some woman with a Welsh name inscribed on the back. And I cannot find the trick to the secret bottom that *Dej* said it had."

"Well, it must be—"

A grating sound of metal on metal interrupted. Glynis glanced at the door, puzzled, and then realized that someone was unlocking the door from the other side.

She glanced at Christo. He shrugged as if resigned, and climbed to his feet. She rose as well. Then, as the Earl of St. Albans stepped into the room, she folded her arms and pressed her lips into a tight line.

He checked at once on the threshold, one eyebrow flying up and his expression momentarily startled as his glance shifted from Glynis to her brother and back again. Then the corner of his mouth quirked, and his eyelids drooped. "An uninvited guest. How delightfully informal."

Glynis flung her arms wide. "Who is uninvited here, my lord? You do not even bother with a polite knock, do you? You simply come in because you are the Earl of St. Albans and it is your house, and you have only yourself to please!"

His expression did not change, but it seemed to her that the corner of his mouth tightened.

"Why, yes. That more or less sums it up," he said. And then, as if to prove her opinion of him correct, he strolled into the room, his robe billowing around him.

He looked faintly amused by her outburst—and arrogantly assured of himself. Ah, but she hated that smug smile of his, as if he found a secret joke in all of this. She did not want him to think of her as a diversion, and a . . .

Looking away from him, she stopped her thoughts. Ah, but what was she doing? She did not want this *gaujo* to think of her as anything. It must not matter to her if he chose to regard her as a Gypsy, a thing for his sport—and not a woman with feelings that could be wounded.

Taking a deep breath, she glanced back at him, chin lowered, mouth set with the determination not to care.

He stood unnaturally still, his expression unreadable, and Glynis clenched her fists, as if she could hold back the hurt that welled in her. This man thought of her as a challenge—a chase to enjoy. She must remember that.

St. Albans's stare remained on her a moment longer, and then he turned to her brother. "I do hope that you at least did not leave your . . . what was it, ah, yes, your *tshuri* stuck into any of my staff. It is the very devil to train them into their place, and such a bother to replace them."

Christo shifted, tucking the box under his arm. "Don't worry, *gaujo*. I saved my knife in case we met."

"How thoughtful of you." He glanced at the box, and then shifted that glittering stare to Glynis. "The infamous box? I begin to understand now. This means that your use for me is at an end, does it not?"

She lifted her chin. "Yes, I suppose it does, *gaujo*."

He came towards her, something hot lurking in his eyes, his movements sinfully graceful. Mouth drying, her arms fell to her sides and she barely stopped herself from falling back a step. He would not intimidate her.

But what did he plot now?

His smile twisted. He took her hand, his own so much warmer than hers, his touch certain and strong. "You may relax, my dear. I merely wish to tell you that I have enjoyed our association, and I shall bid you goodbye."

Her jaw slackened. *Goodbye?* What did he mean by that?

He kissed her hand, his breath warm and his lips soft. She studied his face for some sign of devilment, some indication of his thoughts, but she saw nothing other than a dark glimmer in his eyes which meant that that too-quick mind of his was turning.

Then he let go of her and strode for the door.

A knot formed in her throat.

Ah, but he was not really going. This was just a trick of his. Was it not?

At the door, he paused, and Glynis's eyes narrowed. She had known it. This one did not have it in him to think of others before he thought of himself. This was just some plan of his.

But the knot tightened, and she hugged herself.

What if she was wrong?

He smiled, then said, "You Gypsies believe in luck a great deal, do you not?"

Still watching him, she nodded. *"Bok* is bad luck. Good luck is *kushti bok."*

"Well, *kushti bok,* my dear." And with his crooked smile, he swept a bow, and then turned and walked out.

"Wait!"

Glynis stopped, horrified at the word that had burst from her. She had even moved forward a step, her arms falling to her side, and she only just stopped the impulse to reach out as if to stay him.

Christo stared at her, looking as if he wanted to slap a hand over her face. She almost wished he had. But then that awful moment dragged on and she thought, a sick feeling in her stomach, that St. Albans had not heard.

This was no trick.

He would not return.

And then he was there, in the doorway, his expression disinterested, but with those green eyes sparkling in such a way that it reminded Glynis of childhood tales of dragons who guarded treasure hoards—and who liked to dine on maidens.

"I . . . I . . ." Swallowing hard, she let her stuttering fade. Ah, but she wanted him to go away. She had since the beginning. Christo had their father's box, so why not allow this *gaujo* to go so they could leave his house?

She glanced around, desperate for the reason why she had called out. There *had* to be a reason!

Scowling now, Christo shifted and tucked the box under his other arm.

Glynis let out a breath. Of course. There was a puzzle yet to work through. That was why she did not want him to go. That momentary panic came from a need that she had almost not even recognized. That was all. It was just that they still had a use for this clever *gaujo* earl.

Turning to St. Albans, she said, "There is one thing yet. Since you are so good with finding your way into anyplace . . ." She gestured to the box.

Christo pulled back, twisting slightly as if to hold the box away.

And so she told him in a silent, glowering stare, *Well, why not ask him? Can you open it?*

Christo's mouth pulled deeper. He glanced at St. Albans, suspicion in his narrowed eyes, and then he turned back to Glynis, his body stiff and still holding the box away from her.

She glared back at him.

Watching the silent exchange between brother and sister, St. Albans slowly eased into the room. His Gypsy still defended him, it seemed.

And she had called him back.

That had been a gamble. And there had been those six agonizing heartbeats of silence in which he had doubted himself. His palms had actually broken into a sweat, something he could not recall happening since his first day at Eton, when he had stared at a sea of strange faces and felt himself alone in their midst.

However, the Earls of St. Albans did not doubt anything, particularly not themselves. So why had anxiety raced through him? Nothing, after all, had been at risk. If she had not called out, he would have found another way for their paths to cross again.

But it had mattered that she did call to him.

It mattered also now what lay inside that blasted box. Was it proof to gain her respectability, or proof he could use to coax her into becoming his mistress?

She took a deep breath, and St. Albans braced himself as his Gypsy went to her brother and gently took the box from him.

Glynis held the box in both her hands, grateful that it was so heavy that it kept her grip steady.

At last. At long last. Inside lay the key to Christopher's rightful inheritance. And hers. Now they could have a future. A home. Respectability.

And then she looked up at St. Albans.

He stood close by, his eyes narrowed so that they seemed almost like cat's eyes, flickering green in that disdainful expression of his. He looked dangerous in his flowing dressing gown, his white lawn shirt open at the throat to reveal the hint of muscles that lay under his polished exterior. He looked as if he had just come from his bed to her. His mouth curved into the cynical twist she knew so well. The one that kept others away.

Pressing her lips together, she glanced down at the box again. Cunning carving decorated the rich rosewood. The red and gold tones in the wood had been worked so that the hewn dragon seemed almost to breathe as she tilted the oblong box. More carving, rich and intricate and ancient, marked its pattern on her palms as she clutched the box.

She looked up again at St. Albans, her lips parched, her throat tight. If she opened the box, she gained her future.

But what of St. Albans? He had no use for a respectable lady—not even for a wife.

With a muffled curse, she pushed aside such thoughts. No use to long for what could not be. *Dej* had taught her that. But she could act on what must be.

She held out the box to St. Albans. "It has a secret latch. We do not know how to open it. Can you?"

For an instant, his mouth crooked even higher on one side. *He will refuse,* she thought, disappointment seeping into her.

And then, in an instant, he was at her side, his hands covering hers to take the box.

"Please allow me," he said, his tone drawling and sounding dreadfully bored.

She hesitated one last moment, her mind telling her not to trust him with this treasure. But this one knew things. This one could do things. If anyone could open this box, he could.

Letting go, she released the box into St. Albans's grip.

He stood there, the box in his hands, turning it over. He pulled back the iron lock and opened the lid.

"I emptied that already," Christo said, sounding irritated.

St. Albans lifted one eyebrow. "So I see." He glanced at Glynis. Then he took the box over to the marble flooring that formed a square around the fireplace. By firelight, he angled the box, studying it.

Either it had a very thick bottom, or there was indeed a secret compartment, St. Albans decided. Blazes, but he hated puzzles such as this. As a child, he had burned his aunt's wooden puzzles. He had not been able to get any of them to fit, and so, embarrassed by his failure, hating the things, humiliated for his own inadequacy, he had shoved the lot of them into the fire. That solved them quick enough.

But that uncomfortable sense of inadequacy had remained, even after the flames had died.

It was back again.

Well, he knew but one method to solve that.

Gently, he put the box down upon the floor, the bottom up, the lid still open, so that it arched there.

Then he lifted the poker from beside the hearth and brought its weight crashing down on the rosewood.

TWELVE

Wood split with an echoing crack, and the force of the impact vibrated in St. Albans's arm. Silence—tense and shocked—held the room for an instant. Then Glynis was on her knees beside the broken box.

Her brother also started forward, muttering curses in his Gypsy tongue. St. Albans leveled a stare at him, one that made the Gypsy's step falter and then stop.

At least he has some sense, St. Albans thought, eyes still narrowed and jaw clenched. He was quite prepared to use the poker on the fellow if that knife appeared. And then Glynis's anguished words drew his full attention.

"Christo, there's nothing!"

St. Albans glanced down.

His Gypsy knelt on the floor, a mottled pheasant feather in one hand and a childishly scrawled map in the other. The box, its secret compartment now cracked open, spilled loose a lock of red-blond hair tied with a yellow ribbon and a tuft of ancient fur. And the truth of it struck St. Albans at once.

All of it had been a lie. A Gypsy *swato.* A tale invented by a woman to comfort herself with illusion. And to send her children on a devil's errand.

Sympathy stirred in him for his Gypsy. She had had to learn the truth at some point, but disillusionment was always such a brutal thing.

Turning, he busied himself with putting the poker back with the fire irons, controlling his movements with extra care. Then he bent down to his Gypsy, took her hand, and lifted her to her feet.

She looked up at him, tears trembling on dark lashes, her hands clutching at this inadequate inheritance from her father.

"Dej said Father must have kept their . . ." Her voice trembled and faded into a sharp intake of breath, as if she were trying to hold back her anguish.

St. Albans's back teeth tightened. There were times he wished he could throttle that mother of hers. But his Gypsy would forget this moment. He would make her forget.

Surly and silent, her brother came forward to stand over the cracked box. He scooped up the paper that Glynis had allowed to fall back to the floor. "Nevin," he said, staring at the village map, his voice flat and empty.

Glynis straightened. "Do you think it was meant to lead—"

"There is nothing here, *phen!* This is a boy's map. Look at the writing. There never were any marriage lines. We have been wrong from the start." He threw the paper back on the floor.

The bitterness in his voice deepened as he spoke, and an unexpected empathy stirred in St. Albans. He knew how it was to have the world shown suddenly stark and bare, revealed for the mockery that it was. The fellow's anger about it would have to go somewhere. However, he did not want it going anywhere near his Gypsy.

Letting go of her, St. Albans started towards the bellpull to summon a servant and see about rooms for the fellow. But Christo started towards the door, and St. Albans checked his own steps.

"Christo? Where are you going?" Glynis said.

"To do what should have been done."

St. Albans went to his Gypsy at once, reaching her just as her brother stopped, one hand on the doorknob. His dark eyes glittered, hot and dangerous. The man looked in a mood to do something foolish, something that only a young man with festering anger could do.

A profound gratitude settled in St. Albans that he was long past this age of being driven by his emotions.

Christopher glanced from his sister to the Earl, the hurt so aching inside him that the world blurred. There had been a marriage. There had been! But the empty box mocked his belief.

Well, he was through with trusting. Done with listening to advice from his mother's dreams. Through with this useless waiting.

He knew the path before him.

But there was no place on that road for Glynis.

Frowning, he glared at this *gaujo* earl. He did not want to leave Glynis with this one. However, better that than for her to follow him. As she had said, she could look after herself. She would have to now.

He forced a smile for her. *"Ashen Devlesa, Romale."* *May you remain with God.*

Then he turned and swung out the door, and his smile twisted as he thought how this *gaujo* earl's black devil of a horse was a good one to take him to hell.

Numb cold settled into Glynis as she watched her brother leave. She did not like that Christo had said goodbye in that fashion. She did not like that tone in his voice—one she had never before heard. And she did not like that look in his eyes. He had looked far too much like St. Albans in one of his dark moods.

"I must go after him," she said, smoothing her gown.

Larger hands covered hers, stopping their agitated movements, and she looked up at St. Albans, scowling. "I must go! Christo is going to do something stupid."

The corner of his mouth lifted. "That, my dear, is

what hotheads such as your brother do best. However, he is not likely to listen to reason just now."

She frowned, but St. Albans was already leading her to the brocade-covered couch and pulling her down next to him. And then his arm lay over her shoulders, sheltering and secure.

She ought to get up. She had to find Christo. She could pound some sense into him.

Instead, she laid her head on the shoulder so temptingly near, burrowing into the smooth silk that smelled of sandalwood and musky male essence. Her fingers tangled in the silken cords of his robes, and her feelings tangled even more.

She ought to go.

But she wanted to stay.

Ah, but this *gaujo* stole the will from her mind and the soul from her body.

A sigh—deep and exhausted—escaped her and she allowed her eyes to drift closed. Just for a moment, she would rest. Just a moment.

"He is going to do something stupid," she repeated, worry for Christo still nibbling at her.

A hand stroked her hair. "Allow him to be a man, my dear. And to choose his own path."

Pain and loss lanced into her chest. "What path does he have now? I thought . . . Mother was so certain . . . She dreamed about Father giving that box to her."

St. Albans's mouth twisted and his arm tightened around his Gypsy. "Some dreams are only dreams. And there are decided benefits to being wide awake in this world."

She made what sounded like a snort, but which held enough of a choked sob that St. Albans grew impatient with this absurd self-pity of hers. Rising, he pulled her to her feet and led her to the mirror that hung above the mantel.

Standing behind her, he put his hands on her shoulders. "Tell me about the woman you see reflected there."

One shoulder hunched, then she said, hurt and disgust mixing in her voice, "I see a penniless *poshrat* who has nothing. Not even a father to name!"

"Look again. Look and see through my eyes. A woman stares at me. Beautiful. Desirable. Deviously clever. She has light fingers and passion enough that she could rule London if she chose." His hands ran down her shoulders and then long fingers circled her wrists. "My sweet Gypsy, you saw how gentlemen watched you at the Cyprian's Ball. You have assets you have not even begun to explore. With my introductions, you could dominate any theatre in London. Or you could be the most coveted courtesan in Society. All you must do is wake to your own gifts."

His voice, low and seductive, teased her with the image he painted. The red dress she had worn at that ball. The way those gentlemen had treated her with deference, and with interest. The rich world in which St. Albans lived.

Ah, but could she be those things he said?

She stared at herself—at the pale face, the enormous, shadowed eyes. She saw only herself. She was no actress. She had spent her life learning skills of hiding, of stealth, not of flamboyance. She could dance. But the thought of doing so on a stage with others staring at her left her mouth dry and her stomach empty. And what of selling her body?

She frowned.

He tempted her, right enough, but in truth she could no more sell her body than she could sell her soul. She could not without separating the two.

Gazing at their reflections, her stare locked with his, and she knew then that what she wanted was not riches and power and position.

What she wanted lay in his eyes. In the spark of desire that stirred a craving inside her for more from him than such looks. She longed to twist in his arms and turn her face up to his for his kisses, and to forget herself, and to forget the world.

What she wanted was him.

Would it be so wrong to give in to him? To give in to my own need?

Turning, she faced him. His hands fell away from her wrists, but he stood so close to her that the heat from him washed over her. His scent mixed with the faint fragrance of summer that drifted in from the open window.

The tug between them pulled like the rush of a river— only she stood on one bank, and he stood on the other. And neither of them, she knew with soul-weariness, could cross.

Yes, she could have a night with him. Perhaps even a few nights. And how many other nights would she then spend wishing for him? How long would she torture herself, after he left her, with thoughts of him with other women? She did not want her mother's empty life.

The heaviness of her choice weighted her shoulders and her heart. But she lifted her chin, and met the look in those gleaming eyes of his.

"None of those things would make me happy," she said.

He stared at her, his expression puzzled, as if he had not quite understood her words. Then his mouth quirked. "I see what it is. You still worry about that brother of yours—about what will become of him. Why can you not think of yourself for once?"

"I am! I am thinking how miserable I should be, even if I rule the world, while those I love still travel endlessly. And I think about how you use your money and your houses and your power to please yourself. But you never seem happy. And you want only what you cannot have!"

His mouth twisted even more. "If we are to speak of chasing, then let us talk of your pursuit of illusion. You are a bastard child, and the sooner you accept the truth, the sooner you can have something more than this half-life of dreams that are destined to be shattered again and again. How much pain do you need to inflict on yourself?"

"What I seek is not an illusion. I believe in my father's honor. He loved my mother. He married her! Christo and I will prove that someday."

St. Albans scowled at her, exasperated. He had thought this box would be an end to it, but she would not relent. Bloody all, but he had just offered to lay London at her feet—something he had offered no woman, and she had said it would make her miserable. Miserable!

Well, he was done with the game. He would have her, and that would honestly be an end to it.

Circling her wrists again with his fingers, he captured her hands behind her back and then pulled her closer.

She stiffened. That martyr face closed her expression, shuttering the fire in her eyes, masking her feelings. Closing her eyes, she set her mouth into a line.

With a low, frustrated growl, he pinned both her hands in one of his, and then brought his other hand around to cup her chin. This trick would not save her. Not this time.

He bent over her, lowered his mouth to hers, pressing her body against his, heat and need and longing mixing in a dangerous combination inside him.

And then one tear trickled from her eye.

For an instant, he could not move. He watched the crystal drop trace her cheek. The track of it cut into him as if it were etching a line through his own skin, cutting into him like an acid, carrying her anguish into him.

And he could not bear it.

Releasing her, he turned and strode for the door. He

did not look back. He dared not. He did not want to see her staring at him with wounded eyes. He did not want to see himself reflected in those dark depths.

What the hell was happening to him?

Glynis's eyes flew open and she watched St. Albans stride out the door. Wrapping her arms around herself, she caught her lower lip between her teeth and shivered.

She had come so close to losing herself. So very close.

Her body still burned from his touch. Her heart still pounded. If he had kissed her, she would have surrendered. She would have given herself to him. And it shamed her to realize her own weakness.

But he had released her.

Why? She had been desperate for him to loose his hold, but the moment he had, a sense of abandonment had swept over her, and now she wondered if she had somehow disgusted him.

He slammed the door behind him, and Glynis jumped at the sound of it.

Was that it? Had her lack of response wounded his pride? Another tear leaked from her eye and she dashed it away. Ah, but this was probably part of his game to make her want him—and it worked far too well.

Well, she had pride, too. She would be glad that he had left her. And she would not follow after him and beg him to hold her again.

She would not.

Hugging herself, she made her way to her bed. She curled up with her knees pressed against her chest and the bed clothing pulled to her chin.

Yes, she was delighted he had left. She had made the wise choice. She was not made for the likes of him. She knew that. And he did not really want her—he simply wanted to prove he could have her.

He almost had.

She rested her cheek on one knee.

And why, if this was the right choice, did it leave her aching and empty with the longing to go to him and give him heart, body, and soul.

St. Albans threw off his dressing gown, considered ringing for his valet, then discarded that option. He did not want company. Striding to his wardrobe, he threw open the doors and stared at the neatly hung coats, the tidy row of boots and the drawers with folded shirts and underclothes tucked away. With a snarl, he slammed it closed, then paced to the window. He stood with his arms folded for a moment, then went to the wing chair beside the fireplace and dropped his body into its soft leather. Propping his elbows on his knees, he lowered his face into his hands, then dragged his fingers through his hair and stared at the carpet.

He was mad.

That had to be the explanation.

Either that or his Gypsy had bewitched him, but he did not believe in such nonsense.

No, he must be going mad.

Why else had he let her go? Why? Oh, why, oh, why? God, but he wanted to break something.

He forced himself to lean back in his chair. He was a rational, sensible being. He would control himself, and he would stop acting like a lovesick . . .

Frowning, he stopped that thought. Distasteful as it was, he also turned his thoughts inward to carve apart his feelings.

Could he actually be . . . No, it was not possible. These feelings—the frustration, the desire, the irritation, the need, the anger, the longing—they were nothing like the sentiments he had once felt for Alaine. So, what in blazes was it?

There was lust, oh, yes. But something else lay there. Something remarkably close to caring.

Was he starting to like his Gypsy?

He claimed one person as friend. Dozens claimed him, of course, hoping to benefit from his title and wealth, as was the way of Society. And he had acquaintances by the cartload. But few had ever dared look beyond his title—and his reputation. Only Terrance, in fact, when they had argued their different paths through Eton and then into Cambridge, and still they argued philosophy, politics, and life. Two opposites who had found a commonality of respect.

And now there seemed to be his Gypsy to add to that short list.

His Glynis.

Frowning, St. Albans steepled his fingers, and then studied them as he flexed and straightened them.

Blazes, no wonder everything had become far too complex. One did not seduce a friend, did one? And his liking—his caring—did nothing to lessen his desire to have her in his bed.

But what use did he have for her as a friend?

With a muffled curse, he rose. He could not think straight. He needed a gallop to shake the fidgets out of his body and ease its demands so that he actually might use his mind again.

Striding back to his wardrobe, he changed rapidly into breeches and boots, then threw a cloak over his open-necked shirt. He left his room, striding down the hall and stairs and out the back of the house.

At the edge of the stables, muffled shouts and the scuffle of boots on cobblestones checked his stride. Muscles tensed, senses alert, he stepped into the stable yard.

Three burly grooms—nightshirts dangling over sagging breeches—grappled with a dark-clad, struggling figure. A third groom stood back, lantern aloft in one hand and a horseshoe raised in the other, wavering as he waited for a chance to strike a blow.

St. Albans glanced at them, then said, his voice loud enough to arrest the action, "You have woken my horses."

The struggle stopped. The groom with the lantern spun around, his nightcap sliding over one eye. And the dark-clad figure jerked his arms free and straightened.

"Leave him," St. Albans commanded as the grooms started to reach for the figure again. Then he came forward into the pooling lantern light.

The grooms fell back and St. Albans gestured for the lantern to be held higher. Light spilled across Christopher's face.

St. Albans glanced at his servants. A swelling eye and a torn nightshirt told its own story of the conflict. At least the Gypsy had kept his knife out of the affair.

Turning back to the Gypsy, St. Albans let his stare slide up and down over the fellow, then he said, "I knew you would be an inconvenience. Allow me a guess—you were seeking the use of a horse."

Christopher smoothed his disheveled jacket. "Just taking the one back to London that brought me here."

"And that would be . . . Cinder? Well, you cannot. Take another. One trip such as that in a night is enough for any mount."

The Gypsy's eyes narrowed. "Take a horse, is it now? So you can hang me later as a horse thief?"

With a small shake of his head, St. Albans resigned himself to a longer conversation with this inconvenient fellow. He glanced at the grooms, and waved their dismissal. "Thank you, and good night. Come along, Gypsy, my staff needs their rest, as do my horses."

Turning away, he started back to the house, half hoping the Gypsy would simply vanish into the night.

He did not.

They fell into step as the darkness swallowed them. The moon had set, and the night sky glittered with stars. Scents of new-mown grass and roses drifted on the night breeze, as did the distant bark of a dog.

St. Albans led the way into his study. Throwing off his cloak, he strode to the decanter and poured them both burgundy.

The Gypsy glanced disdainfully at the wine, then took the glass. "What do you want with me, *gaujo?*"

St. Albans smiled, then sat in a chair, his booted ankles crossed. "The more relevant conversation here is what do you hope to gain by going to London? I expect you have some fanciful notion of forcing a confession from Lord Nevin?"

"That is my business, *gaujo.*"

"Yes, well, since your hanging for attempted murder, house-breaking, or even stealing my horses would upset your sister, it therefore becomes my business."

"Oh, and you are so kind that you care what my sister feels? You are a bad liar, *gaujo!*"

St. Albans smiled. "If you insult me again by calling me a liar, sister or no sister, I will take great delight in throttling you. Now, sit down and listen."

Glowering, the Gypsy stared at St. Albans, and the Earl could sense the speculations going on behind that stare. Wisely, the fellow relented and threw himself into the opposite chair. Tension eased from St. Albans's shoulders. At least this young idiot had some sense in that thick head of his.

Now, they would see what else he had.

"I have a bargain to offer you. You want to see Nevin and have it out with him. I have my own reasons to wish this question settled and put out of the way. So, I'll take you to Nevin."

The Gypsy sipped his wine, his eyes narrowed and hard. Then he said, "And what do you get from this?"

"If you are able to get Nevin to cry out his sins, you will have me as a witness, and I shall testify in any court in the land on your behalf. I shall get you your inheritance."

"And why would you do that?"

"Because here is the other half of that bargain—if you have no satisfaction from Nevin, you shall emigrate and tell your sister to get on with her own life."

The Gypsy gave a bark of laughter, and St. Albans glared at the fellow. "What, pray, is so amusing?"

Shaking his head, the Gypsy smiled. "You are, *gaujo*. You think too much. And you think everything—and everyone—can be bought. You think the world is all like you—cold and calculating." He tossed back his wine, then rose. "I make no deals with the devil, *gaujo*. Keep your bargains."

Frowning, St. Albans rose as the Gypsy headed for the door. "And how do you expect to get anywhere close to Nevin? You won't, you know."

The Gypsy paused, glanced back, and then gave a shrug, a gesture that reminded St. Albans of the man's sister.

"What is meant to be will be. And if it is not meant . . ." He gave another shrug.

Such blind fatalism irritated St. Albans. Blazes, but the fellow was no concern of his. He could go hang. Only then he thought of the look tonight in his Gypsy's dark eyes—how much worse would it be when she heard of her brother's execution.

With a sigh, he set down his own glass, then went to his desk. "This is useless, you know," he said, as he pulled a sheet of vellum from the desk and then flipped open the silver inkwell.

"You said that already, *gaujo*."

St. Albans dipped a sharpened quill in the ink and scribbled a hurried note. He would leave instructions with the servants as well. Finished, he sanded the ink, then folded the note and looked up at his Gypsy's brother.

"I was wrong about you, you know. You are not only an inconvenience, you are an irritation. And my only hope is that perhaps I may watch Nevin put a bullet in you."

Christopher began to scowl. "Watch? You are not going with me. You have no reason to even want to go!"

"You may attribute it to my delightful sense of mischief. Now make yourself useful and go to the stables and ask Morely—he's the fellow who was looking to brain you with that horseshoe—to have the coach ready within the hour. And you had best do so, for you have my word that that is the only way you are going to reach London at all."

The dreams came that night. Shifting images that brought with them a suffocating sense of loneliness.

Fretful, Glynis turned in her sleep, but still the images came.

From above, she watched a boy sit at the base of a stairway, carved and dark and wide. He had a single tin soldier, its red-painted coat chipped and sword bent by use. He marched the soldier up one step, and then down again, humming to himself.

A maid hurried past, her steps hushed, her eyes downcast. Simon glanced up at her, his eyes wistful, then looked back down at his soldier. He was not supposed to even notice the servants—they were beneath him, uncle had said. A footman hurried past, taking the silver in to the butler for polishing. Sitting up, he left his soldier on the step. Then he rose, dug his hands into his trousers, and went outside where there was no one to play with either, leaving his soldier abandoned and alone.

With a sigh, Glynis shifted in her sleep.

The boy—older now, still thin, his gold hair darkening—stood before a brick building, staring up at the tall clock tower. Eton. Inside a tremor started. Footsteps echoed on stone, and the boy turned to watch a man cross the yard, his arm around the shoulders of a younger copy of himself. The other boy was saying something to the man, who bent down with a smile to listen. Jealousy, sharp and hateful, sprang loose. But they did not even notice, or seem to see him.

Head up, he turned and started towards the darkened archway under the clock tower. Well, he did not care about them, anyway. They were probably beneath him, too. They did not matter to him, and they never would.

Sweating, twisting, Glynis struggled to wake. Then she smiled.

Her house stood before her. A tidy garden. White front, picket gate. Two stories with gleaming windows that welcomed. Roses bloomed, winding over the entrance, spilling white petals.

He was there as well. Now a man. Green eyes now cynical, smile now crooked, his face grown handsome, and his form tall. He watched the house, his expression bored, as if this place did not matter to him.

Go in, she urged, desperate for him to step inside.

He turned away, his smile twisting even more.

No, go inside!

But he was going. He would always leave. He would always stay outside.

She woke with a startled breath, her cheeks wet and her pulse racing. Putting a hand to her face, she blinked. Then she rolled over and let out a breath.

Pale dawn crept into the room, pink and soft. She blinked again, trying to will away the feelings that still crowded her from that dream. That horrible sense of isolation remained, however, haunting as any ghost.

Rising, she pulled her wrinkled gown around her—she

had slept in it—and she went to the box, still on the floor in pieces. Through the window, birdsong and a soft breeze drifted, gentle and seeming so out of place.

It seemed almost that Christo's climbing in here had been more of a dream than were those images that still clung to her.

Had that been his youth? Always so lonely?

She gathered the pieces of the box, the fur, the lock of hair, the paper, and the feather. She had always thought lords and ladies must be forever happy with their fine clothes and food and wealth. Now she wondered what it must be to grow up a lord, an earl from birth, with something always expected, barriers always raised.

A soft knock on the door made her turn. She rose as the maid came in with a tray that held rose-patterned china. The maid settled the tray on a table, then bobbed a curtsy.

"His lordship said you was to get this," she said, holding out a note.

Glynis put down the shattered box and crossed the floor to take the note, then she spread open the folded sheet.

Her throat dried as she read the slanted, stark writing, and her fear became far more real than anything from a dream.

Dej had said this *gaujo* would betray her—and he had. He had taken Christo to London. With the blood cold in her veins, she knew that Christo intended to face the man who had murdered their father.

THIRTEEN

Fear paralyzed Glynis for an instant, then anger blazed through her, hot and welcome, and directed at both men. She threw down the note. Of all the arrogant, stupid, pig-headed, insufferable . . . idiocy! And they thought to keep her sitting here, doing nothing but waiting! She stoked her fury with curses; she clung to it to keep herself moving, to keep the anxiety of what might happen at bay.

Well, if St. Albans thought she would sit here like some timid, fainting lady, he did not know her at all. And if her brother intended to take the risk of confronting their uncle without her, then he must be moonstruck!

Ah, but she must find a way to reach London before St. Albans could take Christo to see Lord Nevin. And she would stop this folly.

She could not find her blue gown, so she pulled a dark green traveling dress from the wardrobe, one that the Earl had bought for her. She dragged on stockings and boots, and pulled her hair up into a simple knot, and went downstairs to find a servant.

She found three in the kitchen.

A maid blinked up at Glynis from her seat at a scarred oak table, while the cook, a plump lady whose apron proclaimed her profession, exchanged a look with the butler. Glynis knew from their startled expressions that she should not be here, seeking after them belowstairs.

Did not the Earl always summon someone? She could not wait for such formalities.

"I must have a carriage," she said.

Rising, the butler gave her a stiff smile. "Beg pardon, miss, but his lordship said you were to await his return."

"I do not care what he said. I must go to London!"

Impassive stares met her demand, and her face warmed. She saw at once how it would be. They did what the Earl ordered.

Turning, she left them, striding for the front door, but when she stepped outside, she hesitated.

What now? Walk the hundred miles and more to London? That would take days. She needed someone with fast horses. But who would help a Gypsy?

And then she remembered.

Glynis wet her lips. The hall and main staircase had been the worst part—it had looked so like her dream that a chill had swept through her and she had had to step around the spot where she had dreamed that her father's broken body had lain.

Some dreams are only dreams, she repeated to herself. The Earl's words, but she found comfort in them.

Now she sat on a hard, high-backed settee in a small room at the back of Dawes Manor. Books filled floor-to-ceiling cases along two walls, and the fire opposite the windows was unlit though the room faced north and still held a chill from the cool summer night.

The butler's frown had made clear his opinion of females who arrived with their hair disheveled, no bonnet, no gloves, no carriage, and no companion. The man would have turned her away, but she had given him Bryn Dawes's card and his expression changed from sour disapproval to cautious uncertainty.

However, the best drawing room was obviously not

for the likes of her, so he had led her to the library and told her to wait.

She did so, her hands cold and her nerves taut.

Ah, but this seemed almost as much a risk as the one Christo sought in confronting their uncle. However, she clung to the memory of the kindness in her cousin's voice from when they had met in the churchyard. And though he had chattered on like a fool, she could not help but feel that he had meant what he said when he had offered aid, and had said that the world weighed heavily on him.

She knew that feeling too well of late.

The door opened. Pulse quickening, she rose from the settee beside the unlit fire.

She realized then that she had seen him only as a shadow by moonlight.

Tall with wavy brown hair cut short, he would have been a handsome man if not for the pockmarks that scarred his cheeks, leaving them rough and cratered. Lean and long-limbed, he dressed with casual disregard in a baggy, dark-brown coat, buff breeches, and unpolished riding boots. He wore a purple handkerchief knotted around his throat, his white shirt points drooped over it. His buff waistcoat looked too large for him, as if perhaps he had been ill of late and had lost weight.

As he came towards her, his hands outstretched, eyes the color of polished maple warmed and she found herself thinking that she had not been wrong to trust him.

But his smile faded and his step faltered as his glance caught on the damaged box in her hands.

He frowned, and then looked at her, his dark eyebrows tilting up in the center and slanting downwards at the edges.

"I ought to have a quote for this, but all I can seem to think of are questions and more questions. Come, but you must sit down. There is a story here, and you had best start talking before I talk too much. Do sit, please.

And thank you for coming to me. If I had known you were this beautiful, I would not have been so bold. But I am glad you are and that you did."

She did not sit down, but thrust the box at him. "I see you recognize this."

He nodded and took it from her. "It was whole last I saw it, but, yes, I know it. Only how does it come to you, and in pieces? Oh, dear, here is the pheasant feather I tucked away. It was my pet, but father had it killed for dinner. I still cannot eat wild bird, but you do not care about such things. You have your own story to go with this, I expect. 'Thou messenger of sympathies . . . ' That is Shelley, but you probably know him as little as you do Keats."

She scowled at him. "You are not making this easier!"

He smiled then, and a rare warmth stole into his eyes and almost made her forget those marks upon his cheeks. "I know. I do beg your pardon. I am striving to. My mother used words to soothe, and I inherited that from her. It drives my father wild as well."

He gestured to the settee. "Do sit, please, and tell me everything, and I promise to stop my infernal chattering and do nothing but listen."

She did so.

He sat in the chair next to the settee, the box on his lap. And he listened.

At first, she hesitated over her words, uncertain how much to say, but no judgment flashed in his eyes. His face remained passive, his body leaning slightly towards her. It was as if he listened with every part of his being. And so the words began to flow.

In the end, she told him everything.

His jaw tightened once when she mentioned her father's death. And some fleeting emotion passed through his eyes when she spoke of the attack that left her mother blind. But he said nothing. Not a word of denial or outrage. Almost as if he had somehow expected to hear this.

He kept one hand—narrow, with tapering fingers—over the box as she spoke.

And when she finished, he sat very still a moment.

Then he glanced down at the box, and shook his head. "I never knew. 'While yet a boy I sought for ghosts . . .' And if I had known . . ."

Rising suddenly, he left the box upon his chair and went to the bookcase. He hefted out a book bound in black leather, riffling its pages as he spoke.

"I was ten when my father showed me the Dawes Dragonbox, saying it would come to me as his heir. I found it endlessly fascinating. It did not hurt, of course, that father seemed obsessed with it as well—it is a badge of title, you see. And then I found the mechanism and opened it—rather more delicately than you—and I found this."

The book had fallen open, and he came back to her, holding out a folded paper.

Glynis took it and unfolded the thick paper. Fine copperplate writing stood out sharply, black ink on vellum. Her glance traveled down to the signatures at the bottom of the marriage license, and then she let out a deep breath.

Her mother's dream had not been wrong.

Smiling, Bryn sat next to her on the settee. "Welcome to the family, Cousin. You look very like your father. I can see it now. His portrait hangs in the great hall, rather hidden away, I am afraid, but perhaps I shall be able to show you someday."

She looked at him, frowning. "Why? Why would you give this to me?"

His eyebrows tilted up in the center again and he regarded her, his expression taken aback. "How can I not? It was another matter when I thought this an issue without issue. I almost gave this, in fact, to my father, but he was in one of his tempers—as was I about my poor pheasant. So, as my petty act of revenge, I tucked my own treasures into the box, but I could not very well destroy family papers, so I put them where they would not be found."

Glynis glanced at the book he held.

Bryn smiled, but his eyes did not warm. "Shakespeare. My father thinks the only verse anyone needs read is the Old Testament. Poetry is for the weak-minded."

She looked up at him. "My brother has gone to see him."

Bryn's smile left his face. "That I would not recommend. I think—I pray—your father's death was an accident. But, in any case, my father will not welcome either of you. He is a proud man—'burning pride and high disdain'—and at the least he will make your lives miserable if he can. He is rather good at that."

She heard the mix of regret and resentment in his voice, but her worry for Christo overrode all other concern.

She lifted the marriage lines. "There is no need for my brother to have to face your father anywhere but in a court of law once this is in his hands. But I must get it to him before he goes to Nevin House."

Frowning, Bryn nodded. "When did they leave? Hours ago? It is not likely we shall arrive beforehand, but the toll roads will slow them, and if we travel faster and lighter—but are you certain you will not allow me to take these to him?"

She shook her head and her hands closed around the paper. She ought to allow him to take them. She knew it. But she could not bear the thought of letting this proof out of her sight.

Bryn nodded and stood. "Very well, but it will be a hard ride."

Shocked, she looked up at him. "Ride?"

"Yes. It's our only chance to gain some speed. You do ride, do you not?"

Glynis stood. "I can do whatever I must." And she prayed that was true.

In a matter of minutes, Bryn had set the household into a bustle with orders for horses, his hat, and the pound notes from his desk, plus saddlebags with cheese and bread packed for them.

"We can eat as we ride—it will save time," he told her.

All of it seemed to happen in an instant, and yet Glynis fretted, too aware that Christo had left with St. Albans hours ago.

Her cousin found her a cloak—in case night, or rainfall, caught them on the road—and then he led her to the stables. She stared at two enormous hunters as they were led from the stable, and thought how high up they were, and what a long way from there to the ground. Then her chin went up. For Christo, she could ride anything.

So she allowed her cousin to toss her into the saddle.

After an uncertain and uncomfortable few miles, with her clinging to her gelding's mane, she decided that her cousin had as good an eye as Christo for a comfortable mount.

They changed horses at Ross, after crossing the Wye. And then changed again at Highnam, well before crossing the Severn. To Glynis the pounding of hooves on the dry, hard road became an urgent drumming. Faster. Faster. Faster. But Bryn kept the pace to a steady canter, with rests to walk between, saying it served far better than blowing their mounts with laming gallops.

At Burford, bone-weary, Glynis decided she would give anything for the comfort of the Earl's coach. And for its speed. Then she mounted a restive chestnut, far too tired now to worry about her weak skills, or how high she sat, or anything else other than to reach London and have this trip finished.

Her horse followed Bryn's. They kept mostly to roads now. The wooded paths that Bryn had taken in Herfordshire and Gloucestershire were left behind. At last, the green of Ealing Common came into view, and she could glimpse the smoke of London's sky in the gathering twilight.

They had ridden for so long that Glynis had lost count of the hours. Light-headed from fatigue, she took strength from the litany, *Not long. Not long to Winters House.* And she could not help but think of the bath that St. Albans had offered her when she had first arrived, and how she ached for one now.

But soon Christo would have the papers in his hands and would feel no need to confront their uncle. If only they were not too late.

Night had claimed London's dark streets as they set a brisk trot through the city outskirts, and Bryn slowed their pace. As they neared Mayfair, lamp boys dodged out to offer to light their path with lanterns, and flambeaus burned before the great houses.

Gratitude warmed her that her cousin could lead the way through the maze of streets, but when he drew rein before an unfamiliar mansion, she frowned at him.

"This is not Winters House."

Bryn swung off his horse and then came around to her mount's side. "No, I thought it might be best if—"

A crack like thunder echoed dully from the house, interrupting Bryn, startling the horses and Glynis. Bryn swung around with a muffled oath, and then dashed up the front steps.

Struggling with her skirts and the reins, it took Glynis precious moments to be free of the side saddle's pommel.

She slid off her mount to find a footman hurrying from the house.

"Mr. Dawes said I was—"

"Here, hold them," she said, thrusting the reins at the footman. Lifting her skirts, she ran up the steps.

She did not have to ask for directions. Servants stood in the hall, voices hushed with speculation and gazes locked on the broad, circular staircase. Glynis ran up the steps.

She knew the sound of a pistol firing.

In the upper hall, she paused, but then heard the muffled thud of Bryn's booted feet. She ran after him, and then glimpsed the door that opened off to her right.

Please, let it not be Christo, she thought, pulse racing. And if it was St. Albans who lay bleeding on the floor, she would kick that wretched *gaujo,* she thought, almost sick with fear for him.

Only it was neither man who lay on the floor.

Shock froze her in the doorway; then Bryn's arms came around her, as if to block her view, but she had already glimpsed what he tried to shield from her.

Francis Dawes, Lord Nevin, lay on a rose-patterned carpet, his face mottled by purple splotches and his sightless eyes open, bulging and dulled by the lack of any spirit to light them.

Glynis swallowed convulsively, and her stomach clenched. Her hand came up of its own will to grip her cousin's arm. Taking a deep breath, she forced her gaze away from the man who had been her uncle.

She realized then that the gentleman in formal evening attire—the one that she had not recognized at first and who now bent over the late Francis Dawes, his hand over the dead man's heart—was her brother.

Clean shaven, hair cut, immaculate in black coat and pantaloons and white shirt, cravat, and waistcoat, he looked . . . he looked like a *gaujo* lord himself.

And then her stare was drawn to the other man in the room.

Casually, as if he were at a shooting range, St. Albans stood with a smoking pistol in his hand.

"You shot him," Glynis said, her voice dull. She did not know if it was relief that weakened her arms and legs, or terror that not even an earl could escape hanging for murder.

At the sound of her voice, St. Albans turned. He glanced at Dawes, irritated. Bad enough him bursting in on this scene, but he had brought Glynis with him. Well, what was done, was done. He glanced back down at Nevin's body.

"Well, Gypsy?"

Christo rocked back on his heels and shook his head.

St. Albans nodded. "I thought as much." He turned to Bryn Dawes. "My condolences, and my congratulations, Lord Nevin. The shot will take some explaining, but you may leave that to me. However, a physician of some sorts must be called upon for an official verdict of death."

Grim faced, Bryn nodded, then he glanced at Glynis. "You had best come with me."

"No. My place is here. With my brother."

He glanced at her, worried, then left without looking back.

Glynis did not look at the body on the floor as she came into the room. "Now I want to hear the truth. Why did you shoot him?"

"Phen," Christo said, rising to his feet. "No one was shot."

Glynis glanced at her brother as if irritated. "But I heard . . ."

"You heard a pistol report," St. Albans said. "I presume we are all interested in getting through this as easily as possible. So it had best be a bet to shoot the wick off a candle—that will explain the shot and the hole in the wall. The rest is honest enough for the most—the late Francis Dawes's heart seized and failed."

St. Albans glanced down to find his Gypsy frowning at him. "What, disappointed that I did not murder him, after all?"

Glynis shook her head. Then put a hand up to rub her temple. Nothing seemed to be what it appeared. A shot, but no one hit. Francis Dawes dead, but of natural causes. And then Christo came over to the Earl's side, and she watched, her head spinning, as her brother put out his hand to the Earl.

St. Albans glanced down at it, then moved the pistol to the other hand and took Christo's grip.

"I never forget a life debt, *gaujo*."

"Life debt?" Glynis repeated, then glanced at the Earl and back to her brother again. "What is not being said here?"

St. Albans dropped her brother's hand and turned to her. "Nothing you need bother about. You heard the story that you must repeat if you have any interest in ever claiming any respectability for your family and—"

"Claiming! Christo, I almost forgot." Glynis reached up her sleeve to untuck the paper she had hidden there. She thrust it at her brother. Then she glanced at St. Albans. "Our cousin found it years ago—hidden in the box."

She had the satisfaction of seeing surprise flicker in St. Albans's eyes for an instant before his expression blanked. "Well, it seems I have congratulated the wrong Lord Nevin."

Christo glanced up, his expression dazed. "Is it real, *phen?*"

She nodded.

And then, before she could say more, their cousin came back with servants and a physician, bringing chaos with him. Glynis found herself swept aside, asked to wait first in one room and the another, and led outside to a carriage and bundled in next to the Earl.

Numbness weighted her arms and legs as if she had been swimming against a river's current and could swim no longer, but this day was not over. Leaning back against the velvet cushions, she stared at the Earl through half-closed eyes.

"He tried to shoot Christo," she said, her voice sounding flat to herself and as hollow as she felt. It was not a question. She knew the answer. Just as she knew that the Earl had no love for her brother.

The horses trotted past the great houses of Mayfair with their burning lights, so that she saw St. Albans in brief glimmers. She could see his profile as he lazed against the coach seat as if nothing out of the ordinary had happened.

He lifted a pale hand. "Your brother has an uncanny ability to inspire such desires in others, so it was not an unexpected reaction."

She frowned at him. "You knew this would happen then?"

"Let us say, rather, that I anticipated the possibilities."

She thought about this a moment, her feelings tangled. Without his interference, it would have taken Christo much longer to reach London. But he would have gone. She had no doubt that he had intended a confrontation with Francis Dawes from the moment he saw that the box lay empty of any marriage lines. And if St. Albans had not taken Christo to London, would she have gone to her cousin for aid? Would she have found the marriage lines?

His actions had saved more than Christo's life. He had given her what she wanted. But she wanted more. She wanted to know why he had done what he did. His reasons were important.

"You knew Christo would be in danger if he went on his own, and so you went with him. Even though you do not like him, you went. Why?"

His voice sounded clipped and irritated as he answered, "Because I rather thought it would upset you to have your brother dead, and that was not part of my design."

"So you admit it? You actually considered someone else's feelings?"

"No, I considered your feelings. I do not intend to make this a habit with every person of my acquaintance, but I seem to have made it a habit with you."

In the darkness, she glared at him. "You do not sound very happy about that."

He sat silent for a moment, his expression hidden. When he answered, it was with a sarcastic drawl. "And what should I be happy for? For your brother? It certainly seems as if he and your cousin shall work something out about his inheritance, but I would not wish the legal nonsense he will have to face on my worst enemy.

"Or should I be happy that I managed to wrestle a pistol loose from a man's hand tonight just before he dropped dead at my feet? Oh, yes, that was a rare treat.

"Or perhaps I should simply be happy that you have within your reach your respectable cottage in your respectable village. Well, I am far too selfish a person to be happy for any of those reasons."

Exhausted as she was, annoyance flickered inside Glynis. Ah, but this *gaujo* never made anything easy—not even the truth.

"Selfish? Yes, that is what you want me to think. What you want everyone to think. You want to ruin the good in what you did tonight by twisting it until it breaks, and then you can say to yourself that you knew all along that is how the world is—hard and cruel. But you cannot erase the fact that you saved my brother's life tonight. I owe you more than—"

"Will you stop acting as if I am some dim-witted hero? You owe me nothing."

Her mouth tightened. She would have him admit what she knew, no matter what it cost her. With her body aching, she moved so that she sat next to him in the carriage.

St. Albans stiffened, wary about this new tack of hers, disliking her intent to force some ridiculous notion that she had about him. But her hand only sought his and then covered it.

"Bah, much you know about anything, *gaujo!* We Romany know a debt when we see one. Christo and I both owe you."

He glanced down at her. She had leaned back against the upholstery, and now raised her free hand to hide a yawn.

Shifting, he moved his hand out from under her touch and settled it over her shoulders. She did not resist as he pulled her against him. He smiled and relaxed. About bloody well time she softened towards him.

"Perhaps I do not," he told her, leaning closer to her, the scent of woods and summer roses in her hair. Its dark softness brushed his cheek. "Perhaps I have been wrong, and there is something to this fate that you believe in. Perhaps this is how the design was always meant to be woven. Perhaps we were meant to be this way together— do you believe that?"

Deep, even breaths answered him.

She had fallen asleep.

For a moment, he could only stare at her, frustrated and annoyed. Then he gave it up.

His arm tightened around her.

Fate. It had to be cursed fate, right enough. Here she was at last in his arms, willing—and insensible. He could wake her. But he had seen her face in the light at Nevin

House, how drawn it was with dark smudges under her eyes. He could not resist running a thumb across her closed eyelid now, as if he could rub away her exhaustion.

She made a small sound and burrowed closer to him, one hand stealing up to his chest.

Oh, blazes, what did he do with her now? He had dealt with reluctant ladies, prudish ladies, shrews, and ladies who were that in name only. He had not the faintest clue what to do with a woman who slept in his arms, trusting and vulnerable.

His body had demands of its own, but he found himself curiously reluctant to exploit this opportunity.

The devil of it was he had actually been pleased by her gratitude. And so very tempted to believe that she thought well of him.

As if he had done anything.

She had been the one to prove him wrong. She had found her respectability, and he found that he had not the heart to take it from her.

"You will tire of it, you know," he told her, and she gave a soft sigh as if she had heard him.

"We are two of a kind, you and I, and not made for the laws that bind others. But I suppose you must learn that for yourself—if you do learn it, that is."

The carriage slowed and then halted, and a footman opened the door. St. Albans gave a curt order, the door closed, and the carriage moved forward.

"It has to be madness," he told his sleeping Gypsy. "A passing madness. And God help us both if it is not."

Glynis woke to brilliant sunlight that stung her eyes, and a gathering humidity that stuck the sheets to her legs and arms. Sitting up, she stared around her. She did not recognize the room.

Nor did she remember how she came to be here.

And then it began to drift back to her, like images from a dream. The long, hard ride. That nightmare in Nevin House, with Frances Dawes dead. The carriage ride to . . .

To where?

Throwing back the covers, she realized she wore only her shift and corset. Someone had undressed her. She had vague memories of the Earl carrying her—had it been the Earl? But this was not Winters House, was it?

She rose and padded to the window and pulled it open. Below seemed to be a bustling street, not the quiet green of Grosvenor Square. Where was she?

Quickly, she turned and started looking for her clothes.

The green traveling dress hung in an otherwise empty wardrobe; she blinked at it and then pulled it out. Not a stain lay upon it, not a smudge of dust, not a wrinkle. Clean, pressed, it smelled of rosewater.

With a frown, she scrambled into it.

She had just sat down to lace up her boots when a soft knock sounded on the door.

The Earl, she thought, frowning. Ah, but that *gaujo* had to stop thinking he could send her where he pleased, and keep her where he liked.

With her bootlaces half done, she strode to the door.

And a stab of disappointment caught at her when she saw only her brother scowling at her.

FOURTEEN

She tried to summon a wide smile. "Christo!"

He strode into the room, frowning. "He is not here?"

"Who is not?"

"Who? Who else. That earl of yours. I thought . . ." He thrust a note at her.

She scanned the lines, recognizing St. Albans's dramatic slanted hand as she read, "Gypsy, I have left your sister at Dorant's Hotel, not much compromised but in need of gowns. I will send your mother to her there."

Glynis looked up from the note. "What does he mean, send *Dej* to us?"

"I was more interested in the *not much compromised*—what did he do to you?"

Glynis glowered at him. "That is my business, but if you must know, he did—"

A knock interrupted. Christo opened the door, then grinned and swept up a dark-clad figure.

"Dej!" Glynis shouted, running to enfold her mother and brother in a hug.

It took hours for everyone to tell their stories to everyone else.

Their mother had left the camp in Bado's care when the Earl's coach arrived for her—the Earl of St. Albans had had men following their mother's whereabouts for some time, it seemed.

"Clumsy *Gadje*," their mother said, as if she had

known about them all the time. "But what of your story?"

Glynis and Christo took turns telling, and by the time they finished, the day was already fading and Glynis could think only of her growling stomach.

They found that the hotel served meals in a restaurant downstairs; Glynis regarded the hotel staff's warm welcome with uneasiness until it became clear that the Earl had ordered—and most likely paid for—the best service.

Then food began to arrive, and she forgot everything else.

They dined like royalty in a private room, with endless wine and laughter and stories and delicacies so rich that Glynis stuffed herself.

Afterwards, Christo had to tell the whole story again to their mother, but Glynis fell silent as he talked. She kept looking towards the doorway, and then to the clock on the mantel.

Why had he not come?

Then Christo insisted that she add her own parts of the story again.

It was not until late that night that Glynis had time alone with her mother. They sat in Glynis's room again, near the open window. Glynis lay her head on her mother's lap. Christo had gone out to meet their cousin, and to talk with him of the legalities that they must set in motion.

"Everything changes tomorrow, does it not?" Glynis said, as her mother stroked her hair.

"Everything always changes. Ah, but this city smells of smoke and horses. How do these *Gadje* stand it?"

Glynis smiled. "It is not so bad at Winters House. The Earl has a garden there, at the back."

"Does he? Tell me about his house."

Glynis did, describing its elegance, and poor Gascoyne, who had to jump at the Earl's every whim.

Anna listened to her daughter talk, and heard far more than was said. But she only listened and stroked her daughter's hair, then said at last, "I think you will like living in London."

Glynis straightened. "You will, too."

Anna shook her head and smiled. "I told Bado I would be back by midsummer's eve. We are going to travel north for a time. And perhaps marry."

"Marry? But I thought . . . but . . . well, what of Father?"

Anna chuckled and took her daughter's face in her hands. Such a beautiful face, she thought, even though she could see it only with her fingers. It was time, at last. Time for her to find her own path, however difficult it was to walk.

Cradling her daughter's face, she said, "Your father's love was the most precious gift. And his loss broke my heart. But hearts mend—eventually. If you allow them time. And you should always think long and hard before you turn away from any love—it will open parts of you, sometimes painfully. But, ah, it makes life so much richer. It is like sleeping under a million stars, like turning your face up to the first rain of spring, like dancing in dawn mists. And I would be a silly woman if I were to turn away from Bado. He knew I had to wait for you and Christo to be grown, to be set upon your paths. And so he waited. Now that is started. So it is time for me to live my own life."

"But you cannot want to keep traveling."

"I cannot? But that is all I have ever wanted. Your father knew that, and he chose to come with me rather than to lose me to the road. But I know that you and Christo are like him. You need a place with roots. I had to give you that."

Tears stung Glynis's eyes. Her throat tightened. She

buried her face in her mother's lap. Ah, but everything was changing too fast again.

"You won't leave yet. Not yet."

Her mother stroked her hair. "No. Not yet."

The next two weeks filled with endless papers, meetings with solicitors, and trips with their cousin, Bryn.

At his request, they moved from the hotel to Nevin House. He wore black in respect for his father, but he refused to decorate the house for mourning, and he had the funeral held privately at Dawes Manor in the countryside.

Glynis was glad of that; she only wished she could do something in return for her cousin, for she noticed how silent he fell at times. Then he would talk too much to make up for it, and she would almost wish him melancholy again.

In truth, the real work fell on Christo, who had to sign everything, and who had to bear with skeptical questions and disdainful glances the begrudging acknowledgement of his rights. Even dead, Francis Dawes had influence, and without their cousin's assistance this would have taken months or years. But at last, it seemed that everyone was satisfied, and the courts began to take action, although their solicitor warned it would be months before Christo would be called by Parliament to claim his seat and title.

But all this time, he never came to her.

Ah, what was that *gaujo* earl doing!

She watched for him. The sound of a carriage rattling past drew her to the window. In the evening, she sat with a book open on her lap and listened for the front knocker. She almost asked Christo to take her to the opera, or the theatre, but feared that she might see him with another woman.

Her mother caught her looking out the window one day, at a coach that had halted opposite Nevin House. Glynis dropped the drape at once with the uneasy feeling that her mother saw more than a woman with sight.

With a cane to feel her way, her mother came into the room. "Waiting is the hardest thing we learn."

"Oh, I am not waiting. I simply thought . . . Well, yes, I am waiting. Oh, *Dej,* what am I doing? When he wanted me, I wanted nothing to do with him, and now I ache just to glimpse him. Just to hear his voice. Only I should not."

"Why should you not?"

Glynis sighed. "Because he does not want what I want. Because there is no place in his world for me, even if he wanted me there, and because . . . oh, because I am in love with this devil of a *gaujo,* and what am I to do?"

Her mother found a chair, sat, and then said, "Come here."

Glynis obeyed, coming up to her mother. The old woman took Glynis's hand and put it on her chest, where Glynis could feel the steady rhythm of her mother's heart.

"How do you think you and Christo achieved what you did—finding those papers, and your place in the world? With luck? No, it was with this—with your hearts. God never gives you a desire without giving you the means to achieve it. You have to believe that. You have to follow this beating in your heart, and you have to follow your dreams. It is such an empty road without them."

Glynis glanced down at her mother. Ah, but she wanted to believe. She wanted so much—too much, perhaps.

And then she heard another carriage—horse hooves

clattering, leather harness jingling, wheels rolling over cobblestones.

It stopped.

Glynis's heart skipped. Moving away from her mother, she went to the window.

The sight of the golden crest on the door froze her hand on the drape. No one stepped from the coach, but a groom jumped off the back and ran up the steps to Nevin House.

A moment later, a soft knock sounded on the door and the butler carried in a note on a silver tray. He gave it to Glynis with a bow, then left.

Hands shaking, Glynis tore open the note. Then she glared at it.

"I am invited to tea!" she said, disgust in her voice. "Tea! And he signs it with an 'S'—nothing more!"

"You never know—the tea leaves might tell your future."

Glynis glanced down at her mother. Her first impulse had been to tear up his note—if he could not even be bothered to come to see her! But now she stopped and thought, and she knew she wanted to see him, to tell him to his face that if he thought she enjoyed his neglect, he was wrong.

She paused only to kiss her mother's cheek, then strode for the door.

Anna let out a sigh as her daughter left. Ah, but love could be so hard at times. And it was harder still with a child to trust that all would work out as it was meant to.

Glynis sat stiff in the back of the coach rehearsing various greetings for the Earl. She longed to give him one reserved, but gracious, a true lady's greeting, only she knew the limitations of her own skills and temper.

Cold anger was far more likely. Only, what if he took that quite literally and stayed away from her forever this time?

Eventually, she grew bored of this, and began to glance outside the windows.

She had not noticed when city had given way to countryside, but now it seemed that the roads had been much rougher for a good long time. The sun was still in the sky, so it could not have been more than an hour or two, could it? But she began to fidget with the buttons of the upholstery.

She had just decided to let down the glass window and call out to the coachman to demand to know where they were going, when the horses slowed from a brisk trot to a walk, and the carriage turned down a wooded lane.

And then the woods fell back, and Glynis leaned forward in her seat to see where they were, and there, at the end of a circular, graveled drive, stood the house.

Her house.

Just as in her dream. A tidy garden. White front, picket gate. Two stories with gleaming windows that welcomed, and white roses blooming over the entrance, spilling snowy petals.

She kept staring, even after the carriage stopped and the grooms let down the steps and waited for her to alight.

How could he have found it? Or even known?

And then she remembered.

She had told him once what she wanted. He, it seemed, had remembered. And had found this.

Dazed, she climbed from the carriage. Slowly, almost afraid that she would wake from this, Glynis went to the gate. She reached out and touched it.

Solid wood lay under her glove.

With a smile, she pushed open the gate and walked up the path to the main door.

She wet her lips and almost knocked upon it, but then she gathered her courage and opened the door.

The house was already furnished. Lovingly. Tastefully. Glynis walked from parlor to dining room, to kitchen, to stairs, to hall, to bedroom, to sitting room, to sewing room, to stairs and the main hall again.

From the upper rooms, she glimpsed the back garden—a black-and-white cow contentedly chewed on daisies. He had even remembered the cow.

But how had he found this place?

And where was that devil?

Ah, but that man could drive a sane woman to murder.

Then she remembered her dream, and she went to the front windows and looked out.

He stood there, outside, as he had in her dream. Outside the gate, and far enough from her that she could barely see that black horse of his in the shadows of the trees.

A smile trembled inside her. And so did her fear.

But she knew now that it was not him she feared—she never had, really. She had feared herself—her own passion, her love for him. She had feared leading her mother's life, but she wondered now if that was such a bad thing. Ah, but it would hurt if he left her. When he left her.

But how much more it hurt now not to have him.

And perhaps it would be enough to have memories of having loved him. She doubted it, but she longed desperately for even one memory of lying in his arms.

Taking a deep breath, she went outside to him.

He watched her from the shadows as she came out of the house, chin up, more beautiful than ever, but looking very much the respectable lady in an elegant blue gown, with a pretty straw bonnet in place and gloves on her hands.

She walked, however, with a stride that would put a forester to shame.

Leaving Cinder to graze on summer grass, St. Albans started towards her. "I need not ask if you like it—I can see my answer."

"However did you find it?"

He shrugged. "I did not. It amused me to set Gascoyne to hunting for it when I thought I might have need of it to house a mistress."

She flashed a smile that looked forced, and he thought that this had not been a good idea.

It had been two very long weeks, and two even longer days since he had had even a glimpse of her. He had thought that time enough for her to grow bored with her respectability, for her to come seeking him. Only she had not.

And so when Gascoyne had found the house and told him of it, he had bought it for a princely sum—to save the trouble of bargaining.

Now, he no more knew what he had been thinking then, than he knew what he was thinking now.

"Enjoy it, my dear. I am afraid I have as little use for it as I have for respectable women."

Turning, he started back to his horse. God, what had he been thinking to imagine that she might run into his arms, and embrace him, and offer up that gratitude again. He had not been able to take advantage of it before, but he still wanted to.

Her voice stopped him.

"Gaujo! I will have you know that a woman who lives in a house paid for by a man who is not her husband is far from respectable. Not, of course, that I have much of a reputation left me since all London knows I lived with you."

Slowly, he turned to her.

Chin down, she came towards him, pulling off one glove and leaving it in the dust, and then pulling off the other. The smile that curved her generous mouth set his pulse hammering.

"Tell me, *gaujo,* is your reputation with women honestly come by? You cannot have earned it by knowing only how to please yourself."

He began to smile, and started back towards her. "That, my sweet Gypsy, is the secret of real pleasure—there is no difference between taking and giving."

The pretty straw hat joined the gloves on the ground, and then he stood before her, so close that her scent of roses wound around him—or was that the summer blossoms?

"My dreams come true, *gaujo,* and I dreamed once of the two of us in each other's arms." Her hands wound around his neck, and she pressed against him until his senses spun. "And shall I tell you a secret?"

He could only nod, for he had wrapped his fingers into her hair and was taking far too much pleasure in pulling loose the pins that held its dark weight captive.

"It was as if we were one, in that dream. And you told me you loved me."

Burning now, he swept her into his arms. "Love is an illusion, my tempting Gypsy."

She smiled at him. "So are dreams. Will you dream with me?"

For an instant, he wondered if he could believe in her dreams, but that voice in the back of his mind warned him to remember his past folly. He had been such a fool once.

But she felt so right in his arm. So much a part of him that it seemed quite clear now why he had ached and missed her as if a limb of his own had been missing.

And if that was the case, well, had not the Earls of

St. Albans always been best at looking after their own skins?

"There is no need for you to be respectable just yet, is there, my sweet Gypsy?"

Eyes dark, she smiled at him, and shook her head.

He needed no more encouragement to carry her into the house he had bought for his mistress.

EPILOGUE

The Earl of St. Albans tossed back a second brandy, and through the open doors of his study he watched a housemaid arrange the flowers on the central hall table of Winters House. In less than two hours he would be married, and that seemed all the more reason to focus his attention on more immediate pleasures.

From this angle he could not see the maid's face, but the view she presented as she bent to select more rose stems from the basket at her feet stirred his admiration.

"Tell me, Tuffy," he said, half-turning to throw the words over his shoulder to the other man in the study. "Not that you have much experience with this, mind, but you are a vicar, so you must give advice. How much of a sin is it for a married man to lust after women?"

Terrance Hale—slim, as golden-haired as he had been as a youth, with a face still as young—stepped to his friend's side and glanced into the hall. A slight smile warmed his pale-blue eyes. "Well, I should imagine a wife could rightly object to her husband *not* lusting after women, since such a condition would include herself. However, considering your bride's family, I should say the greater danger to your mortal soul would come from there, rather than from any wrath of God."

St. Albans's mouth twisted. "Yes, but it would be amusing to see that hothead forget to act the lord of the manor. I have never seen a fellow grow so stiff so rapidly."

Terrance shook his head. "You have never taken my advice in the past, so I shall offer it now with the full expectation of not being heeded—leave young Lord Nevin to his own conscience. You shall have enough to deal with in starting your own family."

St. Albans frowned at his empty brandy glass. *His own family*. Such an ominous phrase. Hades, but he wanted to bolt for anyplace else on earth other than London.

Then a soft voice behind him called out, "Simon?"

Glancing around, he saw Glynis, standing at the windows to his study. She had come in from the garden, her dark hair down and curling around those lovely, rounded shoulders of hers. Instantly, his mood lightened. At eight in the morning, his countess-to-be seemed to be wearing only a loosely belted dressing gown.

Terrance cleared his throat, but St. Albans could not drag his eyes from his Gypsy. "Do excuse me, I believe there are some details awaiting my attention at St. George's. Simon, try to at least check your impulses to make difficulties today," he said, his tone dry.

St. Albans waited only for the door to close behind the man and then he advanced on his Gypsy. "I thought it was bad luck for me to see you this morning."

"And I thought you did not want to hear any more wedding superstitions. Besides, it is only bad luck for you to see me in my bridal gown, and I am not wearing it."

He slipped his hands under the silk of her dressing gown. "So I feel. You are not, in fact, wearing much of anything. What did you do, climb down the trellis in your bare skin?"

"Of course not. I used your secret stair. And it is too hot to put on my gown just yet, and you have to stop that, Simon. No, I am serious. I must ask you something, and I cannot think when you start to touch me that way."

Glowering at her, he took his hands away. Oh, blazes, was this all a mistake? It had been a year of delirious pleasure with her. A year and a day with him unable to stay long from her side. A year of arguments and passion, and of coming to loathe having to leave her bed, and of having to bear the whispers about her because of their association.

After the third time he had had to knock some idiot senseless—for Glynis had sworn she would attend any duel that came to her notice—he had decided he had better marry her, before he stood at odds with all of Society.

The latter seemed far too exhausting.

And far less pleasurable.

But now she glared at him, and he wondered if this marriage would change all. *Respectability.* Such an ugly word.

"I need a promise from you," Glynis said, staring up at him, her eyes dark and the dressing gown slipping provocatively from one golden shoulder.

He lifted an eyebrow. "My dear Gypsy, I am about to bestow upon you my worldly goods, and to vow to worship you with my body—is there more you desire?"

"Do not be flippant. This is serious."

He braced himself. A serious discussion. He should have expected this, for of course she would have demands. Jaw clenched, he waited. What flaw—or dozen of them—did she want changed?

"You have to promise me, Simon, not to reform too much."

He blinked at her. "I what?"

"I mean it. I do not wish to have a boring husband who turns all prosy on me the way that Christo has—he wants me to call him Christopher, or even Nevin! Bah, as if I had not known him since he was born!"

St. Albans's arm stole around his wife-to-be. "Not reform too much? Does this mean you do not mind if I admire other women, and allow my imagination to stray a little?"

She frowned. "No, you could reform that."

He began to tug at the belted cord of her high-waisted dressing gown. "And what if I bring those ideas that cross my mind to your bed?"

"Well, then perhaps your looking is not so bad, but only so long as you look and do not touch."

"And what if I perhaps indulge a little too much in drink and then come to you, a touch bosky and more than a touch interested in your favors?"

She touched her tongue to her upper lip, and St. Albans decided that if she did that again they were both going to be very late for their wedding.

Then she said, "So long as you do come home that would be enough." She wound her arms around his neck. "And I would guarantee you a warm homecoming."

"Would you now?"

She pulled his hands away from her dressing gown, her eyes alight. And then she stepped back, unbelted it herself and allowed the silk to slide from her shoulders.

His pulse jumped. With the light behind her, thin silk turned transparent in the most delightful fashion. Then that garment, too, found its way to the floor.

She came towards him, hips swaying, wearing only a smile. "Would you care for me to show you?"

They were going to be very late for their own wedding. However, the two hundred guests invited to St. George's in Hanover Square—everyone in London, it seemed, wanted to witness the spectacle of the Earl of St. Albans marrying his half-Gypsy mistress. Well, they would all simply have to wait. The Prince Regent included.

And suddenly a family, his family, seemed not such a grim future. She would give him hellions for sons, and wild Gypsies for daughters. She would keep life forever interesting. They would, in fact, have the most notorious house in London Society.

His fingers circled her wrists and he pulled her hands behind her back. And then he drew her close.

She gave a contented sigh. "Ah, but it will be lovely not to have you leave my bed in the mornings . . . and in the afternoons . . . and in the evenings."

He smiled down at his Gypsy. His lovely Glynis. "My dear, sweet wife, you have no idea of the pleasures yet in store for you."

She smiled up at him. "Then show me."

AUTHOR'S NOTE

The Traveling Folk of England acquired the name "Gypsy" due to the belief that their ancestors came from Egypt. In fact, the original migration of the Rom (or Romany or Romani) began in India. As with any nationality, the Romany language varies in dialect and spelling, and I have used a standard that seemed most suitable to Regency England. To quote from Manfri Wood's *In the Life of a Romany Gypsy,* ". . . the Romany spoken by English Gypsy today is best described as an English dialect that contains a certain amount of Romany slang and old cant. . . ." That has been the feeling I hoped to convey.

The Romany also, by tradition, have strict, internal moral codes, but were often viewed as outsiders, beggars, thieves, liars, and troublemakers. In other words, they received the usual suspicion thrown at anyone who was different. Since like often begets like, such ill will against the Rom produced ill will in return, which encouraged the belief that they were troublemakers. Of course, such conflict is rich ground for a writer.

You may note that there is no mention of the traditional Gypsy caravan wagon, or *vardo*. These brightly decorated, horsedrawn mobile homes did not come into existence until well after the Regency when mass manufacturing and better roads made the vehicle a useful adoption.

This book was meant to end the "Compromise" series. However, there is still Christopher, the new Lord Nevin, and I am not certain I can leave Bryn so alone. So perhaps this is a new beginning here.

I love to hear from readers, so write, and don't forget to ask for a free bookmark: Shannon Donnelly, P.O. Box 3313, Burbank, CA 91508-3313, or send e-mails to read@shannondonnelly.com.